A NOTE TO READERS

In *Lydia the Patriot* we meet Stephen and Lydia Lankford. While the Lankfords are a fictional family, the Boston Massacre actually did take place, and this story of the shootings and the trial that followed are based on the many firsthand accounts that still exist.

It may strike you as odd that the baby born at the beginning of this book doesn't get named for eight months. While we usually name our babies right away, it was common for parents in the eighteenth century to wait several months, and sometimes years, before they named their children. More than one in six babies died before they reached their second birthday, and usually parents waited until they were sure their child would live before they decided on a name.

SISTERS IN TIME

Lydia
the Patriot

THE BOSTON MASSACRE

SUSAN MARTINS MILLER

BARBOUR
PUBLISHING

Lydia
the Patriot

© 2004 by Barbour Publishing, Inc.

ISBN 1-59310-204-6

Cover design by Lookout Design Group, Inc.

Published by Barbour Publishing, Inc., P.O. Box 719, Uhrichsville, Ohio 44683, www.barbourbooks.com

Our mission is to publish and distribute inspirational products offering exceptional value and biblical encouragement to the masses.

 Member of the
Evangelical Christian
Publishers Association

Printed in the United States of America.
5 4 3 2 1

CONTENTS

CHAPTER 1
Unwelcome Soldiers

Lydia was doing it again. Ten-year-old Stephen Lankford closed his brown eyes and let his head hang down to his chest.

Lydia's green eyes flashed as she bobbed her brown-haired head around the corner and shouted, "Lobsterback!

"This is great!" Lydia said gleefully. She rested against the brick of the customs building to catch her breath. "He doesn't even see us!" She leaned around the corner again. "Bloodyback!"

"It doesn't matter if he doesn't see you," said Stephen, who was much more sensible than his fiery twelve-year-old sister. "He's a British soldier on duty. He doesn't care what you are doing."

"Uncle Cuyler says the soldiers are human beings like the rest of us," Lydia asserted. "If he's human, then he has to notice when someone is bothering him. It's just a question of how long it takes." She stepped out farther this time. Cupping her hands around her mouth, she called, "Lobsterback! Go home!"

"Why do you do this, Lydia?" Stephen asked, his irritation growing. He shifted the bucket of food he carried from one hand to the other. "He's a soldier. He gets his orders from a general or the king or somebody. You're just a silly little girl. He's not going to go home to England just because you scream at him in the street."

"I am not a silly little girl!" Lydia declared. "I'm twelve years old, and my father is a leading citizen in Boston."

"That doesn't matter to a soldier."

Lydia stepped away from the wall more brazenly. "Be a man! Do what is right!" She stood there, her feet planted in the snow and her hands on her hips, glaring at the soldier.

The British soldier blinked in the early March snow flurry that fell gently from the sky. The tall egg-shaped bearskin hat made him look taller than he really was. His red woolen jacket and white breeches were splattered with the mud of dirty snow. Nevertheless, he stood with his feet solidly apart, his musket leaning over his shoulder. He was on duty. He paid no attention to Lydia. She certainly was not the first child who had pestered him while he was on duty.

"This is silly, Lydia," Stephen insisted. He stepped forward. "Let's keep going."

"No!" she cried indignantly. "I'm not finished." Lydia nearly knocked the breath out of him when she swung her arm around into his stomach.

Stephen grimaced and leaned against the building, holding his stomach. Lydia was acting the way she always did. She had to have her own way, and she refused to listen to logic. When she did not get what she wanted, she flailed around in such a fit that nearly everyone gave in to her just to calm her down. Even their mother let Lydia have her way most of the time. In contrast, Stephen preferred to keep to himself and not disturb anyone else.

Stephen looked forward to the day when he would be allowed to move around Boston on his own. As it was, he always had to be with one of his older siblings. And considering the condition of

Boston, his day of freedom was a long way off. Even Lydia usually had to have either their older sister, Kathleen, or their brother, William, with her. But on this day, she had nagged her mother into allowing her to cross Boston from the Lankford home to the home of Aunt Dancy and Uncle Ethan without supervision. Thinking that two were better than one, Mother had sent Stephen along. She could rely on him for an accurate report of any mishaps.

Stephen did not want to face any mishaps. He wanted Lydia to leave the soldier alone and move on to Aunt Dancy's house. He shifted his load once more.

Stephen knew he would most likely grow into manhood before peace came to Boston. Since Massachusetts was a British colony, Stephen had always accepted that it was logical for British soldiers to be there. But it seemed as if fewer and fewer people felt that way. Since the Townshend Acts took effect in 1767 and Boston became the headquarters for collecting customs fees, the people of Boston had started rioting the same way they had during the Stamp Act when Stephen was younger. Mobs broke into houses of British officials or anyone associated with the British government. They threw furniture around and made vicious threats, forcing some of the officials to leave Boston in fear of their lives. Even lifelong neighbors who showed a small amount of sympathy for British officials faced the fury of street gangs.

Stephen did not remember much about the Stamp Act. He had been only five then. In those days, his sister Kathleen had tried to protect him from what was happening. But William had told him the stories as he grew up. And now William made sure Stephen understood the Townshend Acts and why so many

British troops were in Boston.

William Lankford, Stephen's brother, was nineteen now. He still lived in the Lankford family home and shared an attic room with Stephen, but William was a man. He worked all day alongside their father, Richard Lankford, putting out a newspaper and extra flyers about special events. Will was hardly ever home after supper.

When Stephen was younger, Will used to tell him simply that he had meetings to go to in the evenings. Now Stephen was old enough to know that most of Will's friends were in the Sons of Liberty. He also knew that many people in Boston believed that the Sons of Liberty were responsible for many of the wild activities that happened. Some even said that the Sons of Liberty were the ones who truly ruled Boston.

With Sam Adams and the other members of the Sons of Liberty, Will spent all his spare time planning how America, as he called the colonies, would someday be free of the British. America would make its own decisions about taxes and how to spend money. Each colony would be able to give its opinion about what was best for its citizens. And King George of England would mind his own business and concern himself with England.

When Stephen was eight, a single day had forced him to grow up in a hurry. He had been visiting his uncle Ethan, who owned Foy Shipping, down near the harbor. Suddenly the crew of one of the idle ships had scrambled through the streets around Boston Harbor with the news: British troops were coming. Holding his uncle's hand tightly, Stephen had run down to the harbor to see for himself.

The large British fleet had maneuvered its way in from the sea, past the green islands of Boston Harbor. The decks of the ships were solid red, covered with British soldiers who stood shoulder to shoulder. Their muskets were ready for action if needed. Anchors plunged from the ships and lodged in the mud beneath the harbor. The crowd watched from the docks as rowing boats were lowered from the ships and four thousand British soldiers rowed to shore.

That was a year and a half ago, and life in Boston had not been the same since. Stephen had always accepted the presence of British soldiers as normal. A few hundred were needed to conduct the king's business. But four thousand! It was as if England had decided to take its own colony captive.

The soldiers had no place to stay once they arrived. Citizens of Boston had already been forced to take British soldiers into their homes. Uncle Ethan and Aunt Dancy had had two soldiers with them for awhile a few years ago. Stephen remembered because his cousins, David and Charles, had come to stay with the Lankford family for a few months while the soldiers were in their house. Uncle Ethan and Aunt Dancy did not want their sons sitting at the same table where British soldiers ate.

But four thousand soldiers could not find beds to sleep in or tables to eat at. They soon resorted to seizing the private property of Boston's citizens. One regiment even pitched its tents on Boston Common. Another took over Faneuil Hall, a public meeting place. Soldiers filled the State House also. The citizens of Boston lost the privacy of their homes as well as the freedom of their public places.

William had explained it all to Stephen again and again. One of the reasons the troops had come to Boston was to help enforce the taxes of the Townshend Acts. Paper, lead, glass, paint, and tea were taxed. The money was used to pay the salaries of royal officials in the colonies. Since they were now paid by the king rather than the residents of the colonies, the officials paid attention to what Parliament in England wanted instead of listening to the colonists. Frustration with taxes that most people thought were unfair led people to take their feelings out on the soldiers.

Lydia did not pay taxes, so Stephen doubted that she could truly be frustrated with them. He thought she just liked to stir up trouble.

Lydia was still busy taunting the British soldier. Stephen was tired and cold, and he did not hold it against the soldier that he was British. No doubt the soldier was tired and cold, too.

"Lydia," Stephen said sternly, "if you don't stop this nonsense, I'm going to turn around and go home and tell Mama."

Lydia rolled her eyes. "You sound like Uncle Cuyler. You should pay more attention to William instead. Taking a stand against the British is not nonsense."

"Calling that soldier names is not accomplishing anything. You're just pestering him."

"It's all I can do," Lydia said, pouting. "Everyone thinks I am too young to do anything important."

"I'm serious, Lydia. You know Mama would not approve of this."

"She doesn't always approve of what William does, but she lets him."

"That's different."

Stephen glared at his sister, turned around, and took three steps in the direction they had come from. He was prepared to follow through with his threat.

"All right, all right," Lydia said. She grabbed Stephen's arm and made him stop. "I give up."

"I'm glad you've come to your senses. Now just keep walking and leave him alone."

Lydia did not answer, but she began to walk casually toward the soldier. Stephen followed, suspicious of Lydia's sudden change of mind. They were directly in front of the soldier now. Stephen kept his eyes straight ahead.

Suddenly Lydia ducked down and scooped up a handful of snow.

"What are you doing?" Stephen hissed. He pulled on her arm as hard as he could.

Lydia broke from his grip easily. She pressed the snow between her hands into an icy ball. Then she hurled it at the soldier.

"Lydia!" Stephen cried.

The snowball hit the soldier squarely on the forehead.

His musket came off his shoulder and swung around toward Lydia. Stephen lurched forward and grabbed her again.

"You little troublemaker!" the soldier shouted.

Lydia laughed loudly while Stephen pulled on her arm.

"If you dare try such a stunt again, I'll not be so easy on you the next time!" The soldier wiped the snow from his face and glared at Lydia.

"You wouldn't hurt me!" She was not afraid to defy him. "You would get into too much trouble."

"Just try me!"

Stephen's heart was pounding. He was not interested in finding out whether Lydia or the soldier was right.

"Lydia," he whispered harshly, "if you don't come with me this instant, I will tell Papa, not Mama!"

Lydia scrambled up the street, giggling, while Stephen trudged behind her, infuriated.

CHAPTER 2

Unknown Dangers

When they were out of shouting distance, Lydia stopped to catch her breath and laughed again.

"That was great!"

"You could have gotten hurt, Lydia," Stephen said. Frustrated, he pushed on her elbow to nudge her along. His stomach was still flipping rapidly.

"You are such a fraidycat," Lydia said.

"I am not!" Stephen said indignantly. "But this is why Mama does not want you out by yourself."

"Just because Mama is frightened does not mean that I am."

Stephen did not want to talk about it anymore. "It's cold out here, Lydia. Let's keep moving." He stepped ahead of her and gestured that she should follow. When she seemed to resist, Stephen added, "Aunt Dancy is waiting for us, and we don't want her going out in this cold because she's worried about where we are. If we don't hurry up, we'll be late."

Aunt Dancy was the reason they were making this trip across town. She was going to have a baby. Charles and David were excited about having a new baby in the house, even though they were twelve and fourteen years old. Stephen was the youngest of all the cousins in the Turner and Lankford families. Everyone was excited about a new member of the family after ten years.

"Aunt Dancy is not a fraidycat," Lydia declared. "She's going to have a baby in a month, but she's not afraid to be alone in her house."

"That may be true," Stephen argued, "but she will be afraid if we don't show up on time when there's so much danger on the streets. Now let's go!"

Uncle Ethan had needed to make a business trip from Boston to New York City. He hated the thought of leaving Aunt Dancy in her condition, but the business was pressing, and he felt he must go.

Charles and David had been nagging to go to New York for months. Aunt Dancy had insisted that Uncle Ethan take their sons with him. After all, the baby was not going to be born for at least a month. It was better if everyone kept busy while they waited, she had pointed out. It was good for the boys' education to see New York and learn more about their father's business. Uncle Ethan had resisted at first, but not for long. He had learned many years earlier that there was little point in arguing with his wife once she had made up her mind.

As a compromise, Aunt Dancy had agreed to let the other relatives take turns spending the nights with her. Uncle Ethan did not want her to be alone, just in case something unexpected should happen—which Dancy was sure would not happen. She agreed to her husband's plan simply to keep him happy.

So Stephen and Lydia's older sister, Kathleen, had spent several nights with Aunt Dancy, as had their mother. Uncle Cuyler's wife, Aunt Abigail, had taken several turns. Then Lydia had pleaded for a turn. She'd insisted that twelve years of age was old enough to be trusted with something as simple as sleeping in the same house with her aunt. After days of listening to her daughter's relentless insistence that she was ready for grown-up responsibility, Mama had given in. But she'd sent Stephen along as well. Lydia had objected furiously, but Mama had held firm this time.

As they walked, Stephen checked the tin bucket of food he carried. This was their supper. The biscuits wrapped in a cloth had survived the excitement, but some of the gravy had spilled during the frenzy of getting away from the soldier. Stephen's fingers were getting sticky. He decided that if there was not enough to go around, he would simply say that he did not care for any gravy with his biscuits that night.

Uncle Ethan had been gone ten days now. In only two more days, he would return to look after Aunt Dancy himself. In the meantime, she spent her days at the Foy Shipping office, making sure the accounts were kept current. Both Stephen's mother and Aunt Abigail found a series of excuses to drop in at the office of Foy Shipping. Aunt Dancy spent her evenings chatting with whatever relative had been assigned to bring her supper and sit with her for that night. Now it was Lydia and Stephen. Aunt Dancy kept insisting that there was plenty of time before the baby would come and that they were all fussing over nothing, but she accepted the attention anyway.

"Do you think Aunt Dancy will have a boy or a girl?" asked Lydia.

Stephen shrugged. "I'm sure they would like a girl, since they have two boys."

"Charles and David want a little brother."

"I'm sure Aunt Dancy and Uncle Ethan would be happy with another boy, too."

"Don't you ever have an opinion about anything?" Lydia taunted.

"Why should I have an opinion about whether Aunt Dancy should have a boy or a girl?" Stephen defended himself. "The baby is already a boy or a girl. No one can change that now."

"Stephen Lankford, you're hopeless. You have no imagination." Lydia skipped ahead of her brother.

Lydia stopped abruptly a few yards ahead of Stephen. "Look," she said as she pointed. "There's William."

Stephen looked across the street and saw William standing under the elm tree that all of Boston called the Liberty Tree. His height and his sleek, thick brown hair made him easy to spot. Sam Adams, the leader of the group, was there, along with a dozen or so other young men.

"William!" Lydia cupped her hands around her mouth and shouted across the street. "William Richard Lankford!"

William turned around and grinned at his younger siblings. He gave a friendly wave and turned back to the meeting.

"Why don't they find a warm place to meet?" Stephen wondered aloud.

"Because the British have taken over all the buildings, silly."

"Not every building," Stephen countered. "They must be getting cold out here."

"They don't mind. They are talking about important matters, so they don't notice the cold."

"Well, I do. Let's get moving again."

Lydia's green eyes flashed. "Let's go see him!"

Before Stephen could protest, Lydia had dashed out into the street between horse carriages. He had no choice but to follow. Mama had given him firm instructions to stay close to Lydia. Weaving through the horses and people who crowded the street, Stephen was trapped several steps behind his sister.

"Watch where you're going!" A man shouted gruffly from a carriage Stephen had nearly stepped in front of.

Stephen searched the road for Lydia. She had already made it across and caught William's attention.

William met them at the edge of the street. "What are you two doing out and about this afternoon?" he asked lightly.

Lydia drew herself up tall. "It's my turn to stay with Aunt Dancy tonight."

William glanced at his brother. "And Mama wanted Stephen to go, too?"

Lydia folded her arms across her chest and pouted. "She doesn't want to treat me like a grown-up. She makes Stephen go everywhere with me so she can find out everything that happens."

William looked at her seriously. "You listen to Mama, do you hear me? She is doing the best thing for you." He moved his gaze to Stephen. "What do you have there?"

Stephen held up the bucket. "Biscuits and gravy for supper."

"Good. Aunt Dancy should just rest and let people take care of her."

"You would never do that," Lydia challenged.

William laughed. "I'm not about to have a baby!"

Stephen liked it when William laughed. The brothers looked very much alike. Everyone thought so. Their dark hair and dark eyes and their tall, slender frames made people know immediately that they were brothers. But the resemblance ended there. In temperament and personality, Lydia was more like William, and Stephen was more like their quiet sister, Kathleen.

"What are you doing here?" Lydia asked eagerly. "Shouldn't you be at the print shop?"

"I finished my work early. Papa said he would stay and clean up."

"Does he know you're here?" Stephen asked.

Stephen knew that although Papa could not stop his grown son from making his own political choices, he still worried about Will and wanted to know where he was as much as possible. Stephen had seen his father sit up late many nights beside the fire, waiting for Will to come home. Sometimes the wait lasted all night.

Will was nodding. "I tell Papa as much as I can," he said. "Even though we don't agree on everything, he is still my father, and I respect him."

"Do you think Papa will ever let you print what you want to print in the newspaper?" Lydia asked exuberantly.

Will's eyes twinkled. "The newspaper belongs to Papa, but I keep asking. I haven't given up hope." He nodded back toward the tree. "I need to go back to my meeting. Give Aunt Dancy my love."

"Can we stay and listen?" Lydia begged. Stephen cringed inwardly.

"I don't think that is a good idea," Will said.

"But it's a public place," Lydia argued. "Sam Adams doesn't own this tree."

"It's cold, Lydia, and it will be dark soon. Go on to Aunt Dancy's."

Stephen saw the look of firmness in his brother's eyes and breathed a sigh of relief. Lydia was not going to get her way this time.

Stephen heard the bolt slide from the inside of the door. Everyone kept their doors bolted, even during the daytime. He was glad to see that despite Aunt Dancy's insistence that she would be fine on her own, she was being careful. *Lydia,* Stephen thought, *would leave the front door wide open and dare British soldiers passing by to cross the threshold.*

"Hello, you two," Aunt Dancy said. "You're late. I was just about to come looking for you. Now that would certainly defeat the purpose of your coming, wouldn't it?"

Stephen gave Lydia a knowing look and then turned away from her glare. He was relieved. Aunt Dancy was in a good mood. The evening would pass pleasantly; he would sleep in David's bed, and then in the morning, he'd go home for a big breakfast. He smiled at his aunt.

"We brought supper," he said, holding up the bucket.

"Good. I'm starved." Aunt Dancy snatched the bucket with one finger and took it to the kitchen, where she hung it in the fireplace to warm. She noticed the pasty remains of the gravy that had slopped over the rim.

"Did you sling this over your head, Stephen?" she teased. "It's quite a mess."

"No, ma'am," he said simply. "We just. . . Well, we. . .we had to hurry, that's all."

"He doesn't want you to know," interrupted Lydia.

"Know what?"

Lydia grinned. "I threw a snowball at a soldier outside the Customs House."

Aunt Dancy looked at Lydia sharply. "Lydia! Why on earth would you do that?"

"But, Aunt Dancy, you hate the soldiers."

Aunt Dancy pressed her lips together for a moment. "I don't hate anyone," she said. "God is not a God of hate, but of love."

"I'm not sure even God could love the British," Lydia said haughtily.

"Lydia, don't be flippant," warned Aunt Dancy. "You are both too young to remember what Boston used to be like. The soldiers have been here almost all your lives." She turned to stir the gravy.

"Don't you want the British to go away," Lydia pressed, "so life can be the way it was again?"

"Of course I do," Aunt Dancy answered. "I hate the thought that my baby is being born into a city that is virtually occupied by soldiers and with so many freedoms stripped away from the citizens." She shook a pewter spoon at Lydia. "But that is no justification for your behavior. Provoking a British soldier could have serious consequences."

"He's not going to hurt a child," Lydia said smugly.

"I thought you did not like to be called a child," Aunt Dancy challenged.

"I don't. But the soldier would think I'm a child, and he wouldn't dare hurt me."

"But you will not always be a child. You will not always be able to hide behind your age, and you may regret the habits you have formed."

"I haven't formed any habits, Aunt Dancy. I just threw one snowball."

Lydia makes her actions sound so casual, so accidental, Stephen thought. She had not even mentioned how she had teased the soldier for so long before she ever threw that snowball.

Stephen took three plates down from a shelf as he watched Aunt Dancy turn back to the gravy. She was concentrating on it far more than necessary. He wondered what was she thinking. Was danger closer than he or Lydia realized?

CHAPTER 3

Emergency at Midnight

Stephen sat bolt upright. His eyes instantly widened to alertness. A chorus of church bells shattered the black night and rushed him to consciousness. From the time he was a toddler, Stephen's parents, and then his sister Kathleen, had drummed into him one response to the clatter of the town's bells—fire!

Stephen leaped out of bed and threw open the second-story window. His nightshirt fluttered in the chilly night air as he leaned out and scanned the neighborhood. It was not Aunt Dancy's house that was on fire. In fact, Stephen saw no flaming towers lighting the black sky—only torches carried by people in the street. Dozens of people, perhaps more than a hundred, scurried in the street to a destination Stephen could not see.

Not stopping to close the window, Stephen darted across the room and out into the hall. Aunt Dancy's bedroom door was open, as was the door to the new baby's room, where Lydia had slept.

"Aunt Dancy!" Stephen called urgently, "Lydia! Where are you?" In his haste he had not thought to bring the candle from the night table in his room. The blackness in the hall was broken only by an occasional flicker from the torches outside.

"I'm here, Stephen," came Aunt Dancy's comforting voice.

As she turned toward Stephen, her candle lit her face. She was just starting down the broad front stairs. Stephen quickened his steps to catch up.

"What's going on?" Stephen asked, taking the hand his aunt offered.

"I don't know, but we'll find out soon enough."

By the time they reached the bottom of the stairs, Lydia had flung the front door wide open. The cold air rushing into the house made Stephen gasp, and he wrapped his arms around himself. Outside, men and boys hurtled down the cobblestone street.

"It's a mob!" Aunt Dancy said. The disappointment in her voice was obvious. Boston had seen so much violence in the last few years. Many wondered if the streets would ever be safe again.

"An angry mob," Stephen emphasized.

"But what happened?" Lydia questioned. She started to move out the open door, but Aunt Dancy pulled her back. "Stay back, Lydia. Stephen, close the door, please. And bolt it."

"But I want to see what's going on," Lydia protested, twisting free of her aunt's hold.

"Lydia Lankford! Do you honestly think that your mother would ever forgive me if I let you out in the street in the middle of this madness? I am responsible for you tonight. You will stay indoors!"

Lydia pushed out her bottom lip in a pout. Aunt Dancy stood between her and the door.

"The door, Stephen," Aunt Dancy reminded the boy, who seemed frozen in his spot.

"I just saw William!" Stephen said.

"William? Where?" Lydia once again lurched toward the door.

And once again, Aunt Dancy firmly pulled Lydia back. This time she closed the door herself and leaned against it, scowling at her two charges. "Both of you know better than to think of going out," she said. Looking at Lydia, she added sternly, "I would like to hear the explanation you would give your mother if you did go out."

"But William is out there!" Lydia cried.

"I don't know what is happening out there," Aunt Dancy said evenly, "or how William is involved. But Will is nineteen. He makes his own choices. You will not go out there under any circumstances."

"May we at least look out the window?" Lydia begged.

"All right, but if there is any further sign of danger, we will go to the kitchen, away from any windows."

Stephen and Lydia huddled at the window and watched the action in the street. The torches lit up the furious faces of the people who carried them. Their shouts were muffled by the wind, but the expressions on their faces were a picture of the words they spoke. Some beat the air violently with clubs.

"Something terrible must have happened to make those people this mad," Stephen said mournfully.

"Everything that happens in Boston is terrible," Lydia pronounced. "And things will not get better until the Redcoats are driven out. That's what Will always says."

"Now, Lydia," cautioned Aunt Dancy. With one hand she rubbed her enlarged belly as she looked anxiously out the window.

Stephen watched his aunt. He had seen her rub her belly that way before, he reminded himself. It was an unconscious habit that meant nothing. He looked back out the window.

Lydia's eyes grew wide, and she poked Stephen with an elbow. "Maybe they're driving the Redcoats out tonight!" she exclaimed. "That's why William is out there. Oh, this is exciting!"

"You can't be sure of that," Stephen said. "It would take more than a few torches and sticks to make soldiers of the Crown desert their posts."

Stephen glanced over at Aunt Dancy, expecting her to reinforce his argument. The expression on her face alarmed him. He watched as she wrapped both her arms around her stomach and pressed her lips together.

"Aunt Dancy! Are you all right?" Stephen asked. He was no longer interested in what was happening in the street.

"I'm sure it's nothing," she replied as she let out her breath. "Just the excitement."

Lydia had not stopped looking out the window. "I wish we could see where they are going. Maybe it's the Customs House. I know they keep guards there all night. Those are probably the first soldiers that the Sons of Liberty will drive out."

"Yes, perhaps so." Aunt Dancy politely agreed with Lydia as she lowered herself into a nearby chair. She took a deep breath and exhaled slowly.

"Aunt Dancy, are you sure you are all right?" Stephen queried. He went to stand beside her.

Lydia finally turned away from the window, puzzled. "The baby is not supposed to come for at least a month," she said. "Mama says your babies are always stubborn and late."

Aunt Dancy chuckled. "She said that, did she? As I recall, you put up quite a fight at your birth, too. No doubt it's just the tension making me feel this way. But perhaps you should help me back upstairs just the same."

"Here, Aunt Dancy, you can lean on me." Stephen offered his arm to his aunt. Next to her bulging body, his thin, ten-year-old frame looked very small, but he was quite earnest. Aunt Dancy smiled at him and allowed him to help her out of the chair. Lydia slipped an arm around Aunt Dancy's waist from the other side, and together they began to climb the stairs. Lydia looked over her shoulder out the window one more time.

As Stephen tucked the quilt around his aunt's shoulders a few minutes later, he saw the shadow of pain cross her face. Their eyes met, and his heart beat faster.

"Stephen," Aunt Dancy said softly, "I'm going to ask you to do something very important."

"Whatever you need, Aunt Dancy, I'll do."

"Stephen, Lydia, the baby is coming."

"Now? Tonight?" Lydia cried. "You said it was just the excitement."

"I was wrong," Aunt Dancy said with certainty. "The baby is coming tonight, and I'm going to need help. Stephen will have to go for the midwife. She warned me not to be alone for this birth. Do you know where Mistress Payne lives, Stephen?"

Stephen nodded mutely.

Lydia pushed in closer to her aunt. "I should go," she said indignantly. "I'm older."

Aunt Dancy winced and started sweating. "Lydia, listen to me. Stephen will go, but he might not make it back in time. You might have to birth this baby for me. That's why I want you here."

"What?" Lydia cried. "But I've never done that before."

"The baby will do most of the work, and I'll tell you what

you have to do. Right now I want you to get some things ready. Hot water, extra cloths, some string. The baby blankets are in the trunk at the foot of my bed. Can you do this, Lydia?"

"Yes, yes. Water. Cloths. String." Lydia flew into action.

Aunt Dancy took Stephen's hand. "You know I wouldn't ask you to face the danger outside for anything else."

"I'm not afraid." Stephen's voice was faint but confident.

"Take the backstreets. Stay away from the Customs House."

"I know all the shortcuts."

"Get your coat and go. Tell Mistress Payne to come quickly."

Outside, Stephen chose his route carefully. He was usually not allowed out so late in the evening—certainly never alone. He paid extra attention to every step he took. Avoiding the street in front of the Customs House would mean circling wide and approaching the Paynes' street from the other direction. Stephen carried no torch to brighten the night. Buildings that were familiar in the daylight loomed ominously in the night's shadows. But his heart was steady and determined. He was not going to let Aunt Dancy down when she needed him. He ran as fast as the darkness would allow.

When he reached Mistress Payne's street, he was far away from the commotion they had heard from Aunt Dancy's house. The neighborhood was dark, but he knew which house the Paynes lived in. With quick steps, he traveled the cobblestone walk and approached the house. Not a single candle burned within. He rapped on the red wooden door and listened. No sounds came from inside. He rapped again, harder this time. A knot of fear formed in his chest.

"Mistress Payne," he called out. Still there was no answer. Five times, Stephen knocked on the door and called out, more loudly each time. Clearly, no one was home at the Payne house.

Stephen heard footsteps in the street behind him and wheeled around. He set his feet solidly apart, ready for what might come.

"If you're looking for the Paynes," a voice said in the darkness, "you'll find them down by the Customs House." Stephen peered into the street and recognized the father of a classmate.

"My aunt's baby is coming," Stephen explained. "I must find Mistress Payne."

The neighbor shook his head. "Half of Boston is at the Customs House. You'll not find her easily."

"I have to try." Stephen wheeled around and started running toward the place where he had been forbidden to go.

He ran for blocks. Stumbling over loose cobblestones, he nearly collided with a lamppost as he whizzed past. The blackness was blinding in some places. He ran from memory of where the streets turned and intersected. Picturing Aunt Dancy in her bed, with her face tense from fighting the pain, Stephen ran harder. For Aunt Dancy's sake and for the baby not yet born, he ran even when he thought he would collapse with the next step.

As he got closer to the center of town, Stephen was engulfed in a swelling crowd. Gasping for air, he finally allowed himself to stop and look around. He could not see the reason why the crowd had gathered, and he did not care. He cared only about Aunt Dancy. Everyone was bundled up against the frigid temperature. Viewed from behind, every person in the crowd looked alike. Stephen began to bump up against people so he could look into their faces one by one. He pulled on elbows and tugged on coats. "Have you seen Mistress Payne?" he asked urgently of anyone who would listen to his thin voice in the middle of the mob.

Then he bumped up against a coat he recognized. "Uncle Cuyler!"

"Stephen! What in the world are you doing here?" Uncle Cuyler grabbed Stephen by the shoulders and tried to steer him out of the throbbing mob.

"It's Aunt Dancy. I came to look for Mistress Payne, but she wasn't home."

Uncle Cuyler looked down at Stephen in alarm. "Stephen, is Aunt Dancy all right?"

Stephen nodded. "She's fine. At least she was when I left. But she said the baby is coming. I have to find Mistress Payne."

Uncle Cuyler shook his head. "There is no time to waste. I will come with you."

Uncle Cuyler and Stephen swung open the front door and started running up the stairs.

"Lydia! Aunt Dancy!" Stephen called out. "Uncle Cuyler is here."

Lydia appeared at the top of the stairs and fell into Uncle Cuyler's arms just as he reached her.

"I'm so glad you're here. When the baby started coming, I didn't know what to do!"

CHAPTER 4
The Baby

"Where is she?" Uncle Cuyler released Lydia and glanced around.

"She's in her bed." Lydia pointed down the hall. "She looks terrible, Uncle Cuyler. Is she going to die?"

"She's having a baby, Lydia. But most likely she'll be just fine."

Lydia and Stephen scampered down the hall after their uncle.

"But it's too early," said Stephen. "Will the baby be all right?"

"If there is anything to worry about, I'll tell you both."

Aunt Dancy's door stood open.

"Cuyler!" she said. "What are you doing here?"

"I couldn't find Mistress Payne," Stephen explained. "Nobody was home. Everybody was down on King Street. I know you told me not to go there, but I had to find someone to help you."

Aunt Dancy smiled faintly. "Under the circumstances, it's understandable." She grimaced in pain, then glanced at Uncle Cuyler. "I'm not used to having a man help me birth a baby."

Uncle Cuyler grinned. "Well, if you would rather have Lydia stay. . ."

"No!" Lydia shouted. She backed away from the bed with her palms held up. "Uncle Cuyler is a doctor. He can help you."

Uncle Cuyler turned to Lydia and Stephen. "As Aunt Dancy said, under the circumstances, it's understandable. Now why don't the two of you go downstairs. I'll call you if I need anything."

Lydia shot out of the room. Stephen backed through the doorway reluctantly. He was glad Uncle Cuyler was there, but he wanted to be completely sure that Aunt Dancy would be all right.

When he had joined his sister downstairs, he said, "I hope nothing happens to Aunt Dancy. I don't think it's good for a baby to be born too early. Something must be wrong."

Lydia threw her hair over her shoulder haughtily. "You find too many things to worry about."

"I do not!" Stephen picked up a poker and tried to stir the embers in the fireplace into flame. He added three new logs. Having a baby was a natural thing, but it was also dangerous. His own grandmother had died giving birth to Uncle Cuyler. Stephen thought he had good reason to feel nervous about Aunt Dancy no matter what Lydia said.

Lydia moved to the window. "Was it really exciting out there? Did you really go to King Street?"

"Yes, I went to King Street. But it was not exciting. It was frightening."

"You're exaggerating," Lydia accused. "It couldn't have been too bad out there. Otherwise, why was Uncle Cuyler there? He always tries to stay out of trouble."

"I don't know," Stephen mumbled. "Maybe he went because he's a doctor and he thought somebody might get hurt." He glanced toward the stairs. It was quiet. Was it supposed to be so quiet when a baby was being born?

Outside, the streets throbbed with the action of the crowd. The people scurrying down the street now were curious onlookers who had been lured from their beds by the tumult.

"Half of Boston must be out there," Lydia observed. She could not tear herself away from the window. "How many people did you see?"

Stephen shrugged. "I don't know." He was satisfied that the fire was going to catch. He held his hands over its heat to warm them. His feet felt like blocks of ice. He had not been aware of how cold and wet he had gotten during his trek into the night.

"What's the matter—haven't you learned your figures in school? Even a six year old can count."

"It was dark, and I was looking for Mistress Payne, not counting heads." Stephen sank, exhausted, into a wing chair. He bent over to pull off his wet boots. Under his coat, his nightshirt had stayed dry. Scooting the chair closer to the fire, he drew comfort from its warmth and light.

"Did you at least see what was happening?" Lydia's questions persisted. "Why is everyone out there?"

"I don't know that either," Stephen confessed. "Some men were shouting. That's all I know."

"How could you be out there for so long and not find out what is going on?" Lydia was disgusted at her brother's incompetence.

Stephen just shrugged. He was too tired to argue with Lydia.

"You're not much good for anything, are you?" Lydia snapped.

Stephen glared at his sister but did not respond.

Lydia turned away from Stephen. "I think I'll step outside for a bit of fresh air," she said casually. She took her cloak off the hook next to the door.

Stephen sprang from his chair. "You can't go out there!"

"I simply must have some fresh air, or I will never be able to get any rest tonight." Lydia tossed her cloak around her shoulders.

Stephen threw himself against the door and checked the bolt.

"Don't be silly," Lydia scoffed. "I'm older than you are, so you can't tell me what to do."

"I can when you are doing something foolish."

"I'm also bigger than you are, so you can't stop me."

To prove her point, Lydia hurled herself at Stephen and knocked him off balance. He landed on his knees. Laughing, Lydia unbolted the door and opened it. Proud of her accomplishment, she stepped outside.

Stephen scrambled to his feet and planted himself in the doorway. "Lydia Lankford! You get back inside!"

"Are you going to make me?" She took two more steps and craned her neck to look down the street. "Oooh, everybody is coming back this way now."

"Lydia, I insist that you come back inside!"

Lydia laughed. "Are you going to tattle to Aunt Dancy? I think she has more important things on her mind right now."

Stephen wheeled around and looked up the stairs. Only empty, quiet space looked back. He hoped that was a good sign. If something were wrong, surely Uncle Cuyler would have called for help. In the meantime, Lydia was right. She had made up her mind, and he could do nothing to stop her. He spun around once more and stood facing the street, but he did not step across the threshold. He was helpless. He could do nothing for his aunt or her baby, and he could not even protect his sister from the danger in the street. He groaned, wondering how he would ever explain this night to his parents.

Lydia's observation about the movements of the crowd was

accurate. The throng did seem to be moving in the direction of Aunt Dancy's house instead of away from it. But what that meant, Stephen did not know.

Now he was glued to a sentry post of his own. He did not plan to follow Lydia out into the night, but he would stand in the doorway and watch her as far as possible. But Lydia was not moving. At least her feet were not. Her head wagged from side to side as she tried to make sense of what she was seeing.

"I don't see any soldiers," she called over her shoulder to Stephen. "They probably carried them off to the harbor and pushed them off in rowboats."

Stephen shook his head. Even Lydia had to recognize how silly that sounded.

Suddenly Lydia began to run up the street against the press of the crowd. Stephen's heart sank. He could do nothing for her now.

"William!" Lydia shouted.

Stephen jerked his head up and peered into the dark. He saw Lydia fling herself into William's startled embrace. He could not hear what William said, but he could see his brother turn Lydia around and point back toward the house. Stephen breathed a sigh of relief. Lydia was more likely to listen to William than to anyone else. William and Lydia approached the house together. Lydia had her arms crossed and her lower lip stuck out as far as it would go.

"Thank goodness you're being sensible," William said to Stephen. "Keep Lydia here, in the house."

"That's easier for you to say than for me to do," Stephen replied.

William chuckled briefly. "Right you are. But try." Even in the cold air of a March night, Will was sweating. He wiped the back of his hand across his forehead. Stephen noticed how worried William looked.

Lydia stamped one foot. "At least tell us what's going on."

"I don't have time right now. Besides, what are the two of you doing out here in your nightclothes? Where's Aunt Dancy?"

"Upstairs," Stephen explained. "The baby is coming." He saw the look of alarm in William's eyes. "But don't worry. Uncle Cuyler is taking care of her."

"I'm glad for that," Will said. He glanced over his shoulder into the street. Then he put his hands squarely on Lydia's shoulders and stooped slightly to look her in the eyes. "I have to go. Promise me you will stay here. In the house. With the door bolted."

Lydia pouted, but she finally agreed.

In a few more minutes, the streets were quiet. Whatever had brought the crowd out of their beds was over, and everyone had gone home. For a long time, Lydia adamantly refused to believe it was over and resisted sleep. She kept her vigil at the window and waited for the next round of activity. Stephen gave up trying to persuade her of anything and let his exhaustion overtake him. He fell asleep on the rug in front of the fireplace with a quilt his grandmother had made pulled around his shoulders.

In his dream, Stephen heard a cat. Actually, it was just a kitten, and it sounded frightened and cold. It stood in the middle of King Street and shivered. Stephen tried to reach the kitten before the crowd trampled it, but his feet were stuck in mud, and he couldn't move. Just as the crowd was about to press down on the cat, Stephen woke.

"It's the baby!" Lydia was shaking his shoulder. "Did you hear it cry?"

Stephen rubbed his eyes and sighed in relief. There was no kitten on King Street. There was a baby upstairs.

"It sounds like a boy to me," Lydia said authoritatively.

The cry came again.

"You can't tell if it's a boy or a girl by the way it cries." Stephen rolled his eyes. Lydia said the most ridiculous things. "I just hope the baby is all right."

"It's crying, isn't it? That's exactly what a new baby is supposed to do."

Stephen stood up. The fire had grown cold again. Lydia must have fallen asleep, too. He added more logs and wondered if he should carry some wood up for the fire in Aunt Dancy's room. The baby should not get cold.

"Let's go upstairs!" Lydia said.

"Don't you think we should wait for Uncle Cuyler to call us?"

"He'll think we're asleep and not bother us for hours. I'm going even if you aren't." Lydia pranced toward the stairs.

"I'm coming; I'm coming." Stephen shed his quilt and grabbed an armful of logs.

Upstairs, they knocked gently until they were given permission to enter. Aunt Dancy was sitting up in bed looking exhausted but joyous. She held a tiny bundle in her arms. "Come see your new cousin."

Stephen surrendered his load of wood to Uncle Cuyler, who was tending the fire. "Is he all right?"

41

Uncle Cuyler chuckled. "He is a she. And she is just fine."

Putting their differences aside for the moment, Stephen and Lydia sat on the edge of the bed and peeked into the blanket their aunt held. Tiny little arms flailed in their faces.

"She's so small!" Lydia exclaimed.

"Yes, she's small because she came early," Aunt Dancy said. "But Uncle Cuyler assures me that she is perfectly healthy."

"And you?" Stephen asked. "Are you all right?"

Aunt Dancy smiled and reached for his hand. "I'm just fine, thanks to you. You found me the best help anyone could have."

"I would have gone, you know," Lydia said emphatically. "You should have sent me."

"I needed you here. Everything you did to prepare for the birth was important."

Satisfied, Lydia turned her attention back to the baby. "What is her name going to be?"

Aunt Dancy gave a quick laugh. "Your uncle Ethan and I have not agreed on a name for a girl yet. We thought we had at least another month to think about it, and we wanted to be sure the baby was healthy."

"So she doesn't have a name?" Stephen asked.

"Not yet. There's no hurry. We want her to have just the right name."

Stephen pressed a finger against his new cousin's palm, and the baby with no name gripped it tightly.

That's right, little girl, Stephen thought. *You can depend on me.*

CHAPTER 5

The Attack

"It's a girl!" Lydia pushed open the front door of the Lankford home and bellowed as loudly as she could.

Seventeen-year-old Kathleen was not impressed with the announcement. "Of course you're a girl. We've known that for over twelve years."

"Not me," Lydia said, stamping one foot. "Aunt Dancy's baby. It's a girl."

"You can't tell that until it's born," Kathleen retorted.

Stephen finally tumbled through the front door. Breathless, he said, "She's right. It's a girl. She was born about three hours ago."

Kathleen's eyes widened, and her jaw dropped open. "Mama!" she called out. She spun around on one foot and ran to the kitchen. Lydia and Stephen followed, grinning with their news.

Margaret Lankford set down the pan she was warming and wiped her hands on her apron. "But what are both of you doing here? Surely you didn't leave your aunt Dancy alone!"

"Uncle Cuyler is there," Stephen said assuringly. "He took very good care of her all night."

"Cuyler?" Mama said, puzzled. "What about Mistress Payne?"

"I couldn't find her. But I found Uncle Cuyler in King Street."

Mama's shoulders jerked slightly, and her fists tightened.

"You were in King Street? Last night?"

Stephen nodded. "I had to go, Mama. The baby was coming. Aunt Dancy needed help."

"And I'm not ready to birth any babies!" Lydia exclaimed. "When Uncle Cuyler got there, I was never so glad to see anyone in my whole life."

"And he's still there?" Kathleen asked.

Stephen nodded. "Yes, but he wants Mama to come."

"I want to go with you," Kathleen said to her mother.

"Certainly." Mama turned to her younger daughter. "Lydia, run upstairs and tell your father to come down immediately. You'll have to fend for yourselves for breakfast." She reached for a basket on a high shelf and began filling it with food.

"Is William home?" Stephen asked, although he could guess the answer.

Mama shook her head.

"He didn't come home all night?"

Again she shook her head.

Stephen wanted to ask more questions, but he could see the double concern his mother already bore for her patriotic son who had been out all night during a riot, and for her sister-in-law and dear friend who had given birth prematurely. So Stephen said nothing more. When he allowed himself to sit down and rest for a few minutes, he realized how truly tired he still was.

In a few minutes, Lydia was back with her father in tow, and Mama and Kathleen hurriedly bundled up the things they thought they would need and left for Aunt Dancy's house.

Richard Lankford rubbed his hands together energetically.

"Why don't I mix up some batter for pancakes to celebrate your new cousin?"

Lydia grimaced. "Because your pancakes are always lumpy!"

Stephen flashed a disapproving look at his sister. To his father, he said, "I would love some pancakes, Papa."

"You don't mind the lumps?"

Stephen shook his head. "The lumps are the best part."

Papa threw his head back and laughed. "Stephen, you are too kind. I can always depend on you to say something more generous than I deserve."

"That's our boy!" said a tired but fiery voice. All heads turned to see William leaning against the doorframe. His face was grimy and his clothes disheveled. His hat was cocked to one side. Stephen thought he looked so tired that he could hardly stand.

"William!" Lydia shot out of her chair and hurled herself at her brother. "If you tell me absolutely everything now, I will forgive you for not talking to me in the street this morning."

Will backed away from his demanding little sister. "I'm filthy. Don't touch me, or you'll get dirt all over your frock."

"Lydia," Papa said as he cracked an egg into a bowl of batter, "get your brother something to clean up with."

Lydia pouted, but she obeyed.

"Are you all right, William?" Stephen asked quietly.

Will mustered up the energy to smile at his brother with his big brown eyes. "I am just fine," he said, "and grateful to be home."

"You must tell us what happened!" Lydia insisted as she handed him a damp towel.

Will began wiping grit from his face and glanced at his father.

Papa cracked another egg and stirred. "Yes, I suppose you

must give us an account," Papa said. Stephen thought his father sounded unsure whether he really wanted to know what had been going on all night. But Lydia would certainly not give up until she had heard every last detail, so William began.

"I'm sure you all heard the fire alarm," he said.

"No fire!" declared Lydia.

"That's right. It was a false alarm. But it seemed to make folks edgy, and they stayed out in the streets. The moonlight was nice, I suppose. Some of the men went into the taverns. But for some reason, a group of men formed in front of the Customs House and started bothering the sentry on duty."

Stephen, remembering Lydia's actions on the previous afternoon, glared at his sister. She stuck her tongue out at him.

"Was it a mob?" Lydia asked. "A riot?"

Will had moved on to cleaning his hands and arms. "No one is sure what happened. Someone said that some boys had been throwing snowballs at the soldier. Or it might be that the soldier threatened the boys. Someone else said that a man passing by had insulted the soldier and angered him. Then there was a story about a barber's boy trying to collect payment for a haircut his master had given, and the soldier was refusing to pay. And someone else said that the soldier was defending his captain and whacked a boy with the butt of his musket for insulting the captain."

"This is exciting!" Lydia squealed.

Stephen tilted his head to one side. "So you don't really know what happened?"

"Well, no, I don't," William answered.

"How can we know what to believe?"

"That's a difficult question, Stephen. I don't know the answer."

"Didn't you see what happened?" Lydia asked.

"I was not there when it all started. I was down at the docks. But I heard there was some commotion and went to see what it was all about."

"With the Sons of Liberty?" Lydia asked eagerly.

William said simply, "I was with some friends. When we got to the Customs House, there were about a hundred men surrounding the poor soldier. Maybe there were even two hundred. It was hard to tell in the dark."

"Don't tell me you feel sorry for that soldier," Lydia said, hardly believing that her patriotic brother could stoop so low as to have sympathy for a British soldier.

"That's enough, Lydia." Papa's tone was sharp, and Lydia shrank back in her chair.

Will continued, "By the time I got there, they were shouting, 'Kill the soldier! Kill the coward!' It is possible that his life truly was in danger. But I doubt that they would have harmed him. He should have known that."

"What did he do then?" Stephen asked.

"He backed up the steps of the Customs House. They were throwing things at him—wood, chunks of ice, stones. So he was backing away. But he was priming his musket as he moved. He banged on the door of the building with the butt of his musket, but he couldn't get in. At least I don't think he could get in. I talked to Josiah Simpson, and he insists that he saw someone open the door and talk to the soldier. But he did not go in. Instead, he yelled for help. He shouted, 'Turn out, Main Guard.'"

Papa sighed and stopped stirring the batter. "This is far worse than I had imagined. You're telling me it was one man against a hundred, perhaps two hundred? That's hardly a fair fight."

Lydia opened her mouth to comment, but a warning look from her father silenced her.

"When he called for help, seven more soldiers came running from the barracks across the square."

"All with muskets, I assume," Papa said.

William nodded. "Yes, now there were eight muskets. The soldiers were shoving people in all directions. I think all that the Boston residents had were sticks and cobblestones they pried out of the street. They could hardly defend themselves if the soldiers should start firing. But they refused to break up. They just kept screaming insults at the soldiers."

"Such foolishness," Papa said emphatically. "All for nothing. No one can even say for sure how it started. Where was the commander of the guard?"

"Captain Preston? He showed up a few minutes later. He saw the state of the crowd and ordered his men to prime their muskets and load."

"He what!" Papa was stunned. "Did he not even try to determine what had happened up until then?"

"The British are not as reasonable as you and I, Papa," William said.

"Weren't the people afraid of the muskets, Will?" Stephen asked.

"I guess not, Stephen," William answered. "They didn't stop. They just kept calling out: 'Let's see you fire! Lobsterback! Bloody-back! You won't dare fire!' "

"Dare I ask what you were doing during all of this?" Papa asked.

"William's no coward," Lydia asserted.

Papa shot her another warning look.

"Papa, I tell you the truth, I was not mixed up in this. I had nothing to do with it. I was just there."

"Why didn't you leave?" Stephen asked.

William shrugged. "I don't know. I guess I thought I would be able to help somehow." He hung his tired head in his hands. "I did try. I tried to pull some of the loudest men out of the crowd. They just pushed me down in the street."

"Go on," Papa prodded.

"One of the soldiers got hit by something—ice, perhaps—and he slipped and fell. He lost his grip on his musket. The mob started screaming, and I guess the other soldiers thought they heard an order to fire."

"They fired!"

William nodded.

"And?"

"Four are dead. More are wounded, and one probably will not live."

No one in the room spoke for several minutes. Even Lydia was stunned by the drama of the story. Stephen felt a lump forming in his throat. While Aunt Dancy gave birth to a new cousin, four men lost their lives.

Papa finally broke the silence. "Who?"

"Crispus Attucks. Samuel Gray. James Caldwell. Samuel Maverick. And Patrick Carr is seriously hurt."

"Did the captain order them to fire?" Stephen asked quietly.

"He says he did not, Stephen, but there were a dozen witnesses who said they heard him give the order."

"Who do you believe?"

Will met Stephen's questioning eyes. "The witnesses are not the sort of people who go around telling lies."

"Does Captain Preston tell lies?" Stephen asked.

Will looked away and did not answer.

"What happened next?" Papa prodded.

Will sighed deeply and continued. "Preston called for reinforcements, and three companies of soldiers surrounded the crowd and dropped to a firing position. Then the bells started going off again."

Papa nodded. "Yes, I heard them."

"Those are the ones that woke us up in the middle of the night," Lydia said.

"There were hundreds of people in the square, people with clubs, knives, anything they had been able to grab. They lined up as if they were actually going to fight the British troops."

"That would be sheer madness. Surely they wouldn't!" Papa furiously cracked another egg, causing Stephen to jump in his seat.

"I believe they would have if Governor Hutchinson had not shown up just then. He came with Colonel Dalrymple, who is in charge of all the troops in Boston. They took charge. I was amazed that the people listened, but they did. Governor Hutchinson talked the crowd into disbanding by promising that justice would be served. He promised that Preston and his men will be tried in a court of law."

"For what crime?" Papa asked.

"Murder, of course. What else could it be?"

Again the room was silent.

"By three o'clock," Will said, "everything was over. Hutchinson sent everyone home. He said a terrible tragedy had occurred and asked everyone to go home quietly. He promised to do everything in his power to see that justice would be done."

Stephen said, "That's when the baby was born. About three o'clock."

What kind of city has this precious new life come into? Stephen wondered.

CHAPTER 6

Argument in the Print Shop

Stephen welcomed the sleep that his father insisted on. After filling his stomach with his father's lumpy pancakes, he had tumbled into bed gratefully.

School would be canceled for several days. The leaders of Boston needed time to decide how to handle the turmoil in the city. As merchants passed each other in the streets, they exchanged whatever information they had about the events of the previous night. Horses clip-clopped on the cobblestones as Boston came to life for a new day. Before long, anyone who had not already heard the news would learn of the tragedy, and Boston would rally against the British once again.

Stephen, however, had no strength left. He slept deeply. William was sound asleep next to him. Lydia was in the next room pretending that she was not tired, but in only a few minutes, the sounds of her thrashing stopped. They slept for several hours.

Stephen dreamed of mewing cats and the red tongues of angry wolves anxious for their prey. He awoke when he heard Will moving about their room. The cabinet door creaked as Will opened it to rummage for clean breeches. Stephen rolled over and rubbed his eyes, blinking at his older brother.

"Where are you going?" Stephen asked sleepily. He put his hand over his mouth to cover a yawn.

"To the print shop." Will's voice was almost a whisper. "I didn't mean to wake you. But I promised Papa I would not miss work because of my. . .activities."

"You mean, because you've been with the Sons of Liberty."

William grinned sheepishly. "I should stop treating you like an infant. You know as well as anyone else in the family what I'm involved in, don't you?"

Stephen sat up and smiled. "You're the only one who doesn't treat me like a baby."

"Well, you are the youngest in the family." Will stepped into his breeches.

"Lydia is only two years older than I am, but she acts like she's a grown-up and I'm a child."

Will chuckled. "Lydia certainly has a mind of her own. You are far more patient with her than I would be."

"She just doesn't think about things before she says them." Stephen swung his legs over the side of the bed. His toes scrunched up when they hit the cold wooden planks of the floor.

Will snatched a shirt off a hook and pulled it over his head.

"Can I come with you?" Stephen asked.

"To the shop? I thought you didn't like the shop. You always seem to head for Uncle Cuyler's clinic."

Stephen shrugged. "There's no school. I don't feel like staying in the house all day when so much is happening."

"Are you sure you don't want to go back to sleep?"

Stephen shook his head. "I'm not sleepy anymore." He did not mention the wolves in his dream. He was afraid that if he tried to go back to sleep, the wolves would howl through the darkness behind his eyes.

"You know, of course, that we'll have to wake Lydia and take her with us," Will said.

Stephen grimaced. "I know. Papa won't want her to be home alone. She won't want to stay put anyway, once she wakes up. She would make me go somewhere with her."

"She's good at getting her way, of that I am certain."

"Mostly, she wants to be like you."

William stopped and looked thoughtfully at Stephen. "Do you really think so?"

Stephen nodded. "All she ever talks about is what William thinks and what William is doing."

"She should stick to working on her posture."

Stephen laughed.

William threw a shirt at Stephen. "Get dressed, young man. We leave in ten minutes."

When the trio reached the print shop, their father was hard at work at his great walnut desk. To Stephen's delight, Uncle Cuyler and his daughter Anna were in the shop. Anna was busy spinning a top on the wooden counter. Stephen joined her. Lydia perched on a stool and pretended to be bored, while William struck up a conversation with their father.

"What are you working on, Papa?"

"I'm finishing up a story about the events of last night."

"I could have done that for you," William offered. "I was there. I saw as much as anyone did."

Papa shook his head and sighed. "It seems that even the eye-witnesses cannot agree on what they saw." He gestured at the pile of papers on his desk, his notes from several interviews. "You yourself said that people had many different ideas about what started the riot in King Street."

"I told you everything I know this morning," William said. "I know I did not hear every word that was spoken, but I have given you an accurate account of what happened."

Papa glanced up at his brother-in-law. "Your uncle has a slightly different version."

William turned to his uncle, puzzled. "You were there? I didn't see you."

"Nor I you. But I was there—at least until I stumbled upon Stephen searching for Mistress Payne."

"Then you left. You did not see everything."

"No," Uncle Cuyler admitted. "I did not see everything. But I saw enough."

Something about Uncle Cuyler's tone of voice made Stephen stop the top and glance at his cousin. This would not be the first time that William had argued with Uncle Cuyler about political events. Uncle Cuyler usually tried not to argue, but William could not help trying to convince people to agree with him. William could persuade many people of many things. But Uncle Cuyler was not so easy to convince.

Uncle Cuyler was sympathetic to the British Parliament's need for more income. As long as the colonies were receiving the protection of the British Empire, he felt it was reasonable for the colonies to contribute to the cost of running the empire. He certainly did not want the colonies to break off their relationship with England. Life would become far more difficult. The colonies simply were not able to manufacture everything they needed for themselves. Their lives would not be as organized and comfortable without the support and protection of England.

In many ways, life in the colonies was no different than life in England—at least, it hadn't been until people had started to boycott British goods. They were already finding out that life was harder and the products much less pleasing when they tried to make do with what they could manufacture themselves. When Anna needed a new dress, Aunt Abigail sewed one from coarse cloth that she had woven herself instead of the fine fabrics of Europe. It was difficult to buy fabric from Europe, and if Aunt Abigail had dared use European fabric, she would have been ridiculed in the streets. Many people had also learned to drink coffee rather than buy British tea and pay a tax for it.

England provided many things that the colonies could not provide for themselves. Uncle Cuyler was firmly convinced that being part of the British Empire was the best thing for Massachusetts.

William, on the other hand, thought that British goods were only an excuse for Parliament to interfere in the lives of the colonists at every opportunity. The reason the colonies could not manufacture the things they needed was because Parliament had forbidden it. The British troops were not in Boston to protect the city, but to control it. If Boston accepted the taxes that the king had signed into law, money that belonged in Massachusetts would go to fatten someone's bank account in England. William had no doubt that it was time for the colonies to break free. Sooner or later, he was convinced, it would happen.

"I'm telling you, Papa," William said insistently. "I can write that story. You need no other witnesses."

"You said the shooting last night was murder," Papa said slowly. "In Cuyler's opinion, it was rightful self-defense—or maybe even an accident."

"Self-defense!" William slammed an open hand down on the counter. "No man in that crowd had a musket."

"A gun is not the only thing that can kill a man," Uncle Cuyler retorted. "They were pressing in on the soldier in great numbers. They refused to disperse. If only one man had chosen to swing a club—and I saw many who would have done so gladly—the soldier could have been mortally wounded. Yes, it was self-defense."

"It was murder!" William insisted. "Even if one sentry was in danger, when the rest of the troop came, the crowd was clearly overpowered. Captain Preston had no right to order his men to fire."

"Are you sure that he did?" Uncle Cuyler asked. "Did you hear the words come out of his mouth?"

"It was impossible to hear anything in the middle of a riot."

"That is exactly my point," Uncle Cuyler said evenly. "How could you have known whether the captain gave the order?"

"And how can you be sure he did not?" William retorted. "You were gone by then to birth Aunt Dancy's baby."

Stephen listened to his brother and then his uncle, back and forth. He did not know what to believe. Neither William nor Uncle Cuyler was someone who would tell an outright lie. But they could not both be right, not in this situation.

Lydia slid off her stool and kicked the side of Anna's shoe. "Your father was not there," she whispered ferociously. "Why doesn't he stop trying to tell everyone what to think?"

"Lydia!" Stephen protested as loudly as he dared. "Leave Anna alone. She has nothing to do with this argument. It's between William and Uncle Cuyler."

Anna looked at him with grateful eyes. Stephen and Anna understood each other. In many ways, he was closer to Anna than he was to his own sisters. They were the same age, and they got along well, no matter what they were doing. He could not remember ever having an argument with Anna.

"You're just defending her because you agree with Uncle Cuyler!" Lydia snapped. "You should try paying attention to your own brother once in a while. Then you might understand politics a little better."

"I understand politics as well as you do."

"If you understood politics, you would know William is right."

"Stop it, Lydia," Anna warned.

Lydia folded her arms across her chest and stared spitefully at her little brother. "You were there last night in front of the Customs House, and you couldn't even figure out what was going on."

"I was worried about Aunt Dancy. I was trying to find help!"

"Ha! You cannot tell a Loyalist from a Patriot from a Lobsterback!"

"Lydia Lankford, you take that back!" Without realizing it, Stephen had raised his voice. Stephen had had a long night and not enough sleep. Not more than an hour ago, William had commented on his patience with Lydia. But his patience was wearing thin now. His brown eyes narrowed as he glared at his sister.

"What's going on over there?" Papa took a step toward his two youngest children.

Lydia and Stephen continued to glare at each other.

"I'll not have all this bickering in my shop," Papa declared. "First it is Uncle Cuyler and William, and then Lydia and Stephen. This is a print shop. I am a businessman, not an assemblyman. I have a story to write for today's edition of the newspaper. I have several sources to draw on—all of them reliable—and I will write the story as fairly as possible."

No one spoke for a moment.

"Richard, I am very sorry for my behavior," Uncle Cuyler said contritely. "I should have exercised more self-control."

"I'm sorry, too, Papa," Will muttered.

Papa's eyes flashed at the children.

Stephen swallowed the lump in his throat. "Please forgive me, Papa. I did not mean to lose my temper."

All eyes turned on Lydia. She huffed haughtily and looked the other way.

"Lydia," warned Papa.

"I'm sorry, Papa," she said reluctantly.

"I think you owe Stephen an apology as well."

Lydia clamped her teeth together and grunted, "I'm sorry."

"Thank you, all," Papa said. "And from now on, keep your brawling in the streets, please." He turned back to his desk. "William, we have work to do."

"Yes, Papa." William reached for the leather apron he wore when he worked the press.

"I'll be on my way," Uncle Cuyler said. "Patrick Carr is in my clinic. Abigail is tending him, but I promised I would be back soon."

"Patrick Carr!" Lydia burst out. "He was one of the men who was shot."

Stephen studied the concern in his uncle's face. "Is he going to be all right, Uncle Cuyler?"

Uncle Cuyler sighed and shook his head. "He was wounded very badly. Four men have already died. I hope that he will not be the fifth."

"Can I go with you, Uncle Cuyler?" Stephen asked.

"To the clinic?"

Stephen nodded.

"Certainly. I can always use another assistant."

"I'm going to stay here and help William," Lydia declared.

Stephen looked at Anna and gave a weak smile. No doubt the clinic would be a more peaceful place to spend the day.

CHAPTER 7

The Patient

Walking a few steps ahead of Uncle Cuyler and Anna, Stephen pushed open the clinic door and peeked in. Aunt Abigail moved around the clinic quietly and efficiently. As she straightened supplies and swept the floor, she often glanced at the patient lying on the cot in the center of the room. He lay still, his breathing fast and shallow.

After Patrick Carr had been shot—while Uncle Cuyler was delivering his new niece—men had carried him to the clinic. Several doctors spent the rest of the night with him. Aunt Abigail often helped Uncle Cuyler in the clinic, but taking care of someone as ill as Patrick Carr made her nervous. Gently, she lifted the quilt to check his bandage and tucked the quilt around his neck again.

Uncle Cuyler and Anna nudged Stephen from behind, and the threesome entered. Uncle Cuyler hung his coat on a hook and motioned that the children should sit on two three-legged wooden stools near the wall. Stephen was content to watch from that distance.

He liked coming to the clinic to visit Uncle Cuyler even when Anna was not there. Uncle Cuyler often remarked that there was a great deal about the human body that doctors did not yet understand. Even so, Stephen was impressed with Uncle Cuyler's knowledge. Occasionally he was allowed to hand his uncle a bandage or something to clean a wound. Today, though, he knew he would only watch from his stool. Before him was the evidence of last night's horror.

Stephen wished he could remember only the joyous birth cry of his new cousin. Instead, his memory of her birth would always be mingled with the scenes he had witnessed as he ran through the streets of Boston in the dark. And now this image of a man lying wounded and bleeding in a doctor's office would haunt him. For a split second, he tried to imagine the four men who had fallen dead in King Street during the previous night's chaos. But the image was too horrible, and he chased it away before the wolves could come.

Stephen looked over at Anna and smiled slightly.

"Mr. Carr looks very sick," Stephen whispered. "I hope your papa can help him."

"If anyone can help him, my father can," Anna answered confidently. She pushed her hood back and let her yellow curls frame her face. Stephen was glad to have Anna with him. She was so different from Lydia. When he was with Anna, he did not have to be careful about everything he said. She would never fling his words back in his face.

Stephen watched as Aunt Abigail approached her husband.

"I'm glad you're here," Aunt Abigail said quietly. "The other doctor had to leave to see his own patients, and I believe there is little I can do to help Patrick Carr. You're the doctor, not I."

Uncle Cuyler looked at his wife gratefully, tenderly. "You have done your best to keep him comfortable. That is a great deal."

Uncle Cuyler felt for Patrick Carr's pulse and laid his hand against the pale forehead to judge the fever. He murmured something to Aunt Abigail, who nodded in response and opened a cabinet for a fresh bandage.

While Uncle Cuyler changed the dressing on the wound, Stephen observed his uncle. The haggard lines of his face announced that he had not been to bed during the night for even a few hours. Uncle Cuyler had gone straight from Aunt Dancy's house to the crisis of Patrick Carr. Mr. Carr would need constant attention, so the team of doctors who had cared for him during the night had set up a schedule to make sure a doctor was always available for him. It was Uncle Cuyler's turn. Sleep would have to wait. Uncle Cuyler blinked back the fatigue from his eyes.

Stephen leaned over and whispered to Anna, "Do you know Mr. Carr?"

Anna nodded. "He came to see my father a few times. We would greet each other in the street."

"He looks like a nice man."

"He is. I'm sorry he got hurt."

"I'm sorry anyone got hurt," Stephen said.

They were silent again as they watched Uncle Cuyler and Aunt Abigail work.

Finally, Aunt Abigail walked toward them, wiping her hands on her apron.

"Anna, perhaps we should be going home. Stephen, you are welcome to come and spend the day if you'd like."

"Thank you, Aunt Abigail, but I think I'd like to stay here."

"Uncle Cuyler will be working very hard. Mr. Carr is quite ill."

"That's all right. I like to watch."

"Does your father know where you are?"

"Yes, ma'am."

"All right, then. Come, Anna, let's go home and clean up. Then we'll go see the new baby."

Stephen smiled at the thought of his new cousin. "She's very beautiful."

"I can't wait to see her," Anna said, clearly excited.

"I do hope they give her a name soon," Aunt Abigail said, chuckling. "But so many times parents wait for months before they decide on a name."

They left, and Stephen was alone with his thoughts while Uncle Cuyler tended his patient. The clinic took up several rooms on the first floor of a building near the center of Boston. Stephen was sitting in the main room, where Uncle Cuyler kept his supplies and examined patients. The walls were lined with cupboards filled with bandages, bedding, alcohol, herbs, and other potions that Uncle Cuyler mixed up for his patients. Uncle Cuyler had once let Stephen watch a bloodletting procedure on a man with malaria. Stephen was not sure he understood how bloodletting would help cure the illness, but still he was fascinated by medicine.

Behind the main room were two rooms. One was a small room where Uncle Cuyler kept a supply of wood for the fire he always kept burning, and the other room, more finely finished, was where he studied. Bookshelves lined the walls.

Uncle Cuyler liked to read just about any kind of book: Shakespeare's plays, the Bible, science textbooks. Of course, he especially enjoyed anything that had to do with medicine. He kept every medical book he had ever studied. It seemed like a lot of books to Stephen, but Uncle Cuyler insisted there could never be too many medical books.

Recently he had begun loaning books to Stephen. Many of them were too difficult for Stephen to understand. But he wanted to learn, so he studied them for hours, reading each paragraph over and over until he began to understand it. The volumes that illustrated human anatomy interested him the most. Stephen often thought that he might like to learn to be a doctor someday. Uncle Cuyler could teach him everything he knew, and then they could work together.

Uncle Cuyler sank down on the stool next to Stephen and sighed heavily. Stephen turned his eyes to his uncle's face and studied it. Uncle Cuyler looked more worried than tired.

"Will he be all right, Uncle Cuyler?" Stephen asked. His voice was hardly more than a whisper.

"I don't know for sure, but right now I would say that probably he will not recover."

"Oh, Uncle Cuyler, can't you do anything else for him?"

"The other doctors were with him all night. We have done everything we can. The wounds are extensive."

"I don't want anyone else to die," Stephen said mournfully.

"I don't either. But we are living in a time of madness, Stephen. I fear that many more people will lie in my clinic wounded by British muskets before this is all over."

"Lydia doesn't think it's madness. She think it's exciting."

"Lydia has always been an excitable child."

"She doesn't think she's a child either."

Uncle Cuyler chuckled. "Twelve years old is such an in-between age. But I don't think Lydia realizes the seriousness of what is happening in Boston—and all over the colonies. Perhaps if she were here and saw Patrick Carr herself, she would think differently."

Stephen shook his head. "Lydia would never come here to see Patrick Carr. She thinks William knows everything. Whatever he says, she thinks it's right. Like last night. She wasn't there. And even though you were there for part of the time, she believes everything William says and nothing you say."

"Don't forget that you were there yourself for a few minutes."

Stephen hung his head. "Lydia says I'm good for nothing because I didn't try to see what was happening. But I was worried about Aunt Dancy."

Uncle Cuyler put one arm around Stephen's thin shoulders. "You did the right thing, Stephen. I know Lydia is older than you are and she likes to tell you what to do, but you have a mind of your own. And it's a very fine mind, I think."

Stephen smiled shyly. "Do you really think so?"

"Yes, I do."

A moan from the cot drew Uncle Cuyler's attention away from their conversation. He jumped off the stool and ran across the room as Patrick Carr began to thrash around on the cot.

"Stephen!" Uncle Cuyler called. "Help me keep him still. He'll tear open his wound."

Stephen knew what to do. He had done this before with his uncle. He placed his hands firmly on the shoulders of the patient and let all his weight bear down. Uncle Cuyler held Patrick Carr's ankles, and in a few moments, the patient was quiet again. Uncle Cuyler pulled back the quilt to inspect the wound once more.

"He's bleeding again, Stephen. I'll need fresh bandages—lots of them."

Without hesitation, Stephen went to the correct cupboard and pulled out a handful of bandages. He rushed back to the cot. Uncle Cuyler began trying to soak up the leaking blood.

"He's lost far too much blood," Uncle Cuyler said somberly.

"He looks hot," Stephen observed.

"His fever is raging again. We don't seem to be able to stop it."

A lump rose in Stephen's throat. Uncle Cuyler finally stopped the flow of blood and rebandaged the wound.

"Uncle Cuyler, if he dies. . .will it be. . .murder?"

"What do you think, Stephen?"

"William would say it is, but you say it isn't."

"And what do you think?" Uncle Cuyler repeated.

Stephen backed away from the cot toward his stool. "I don't know what to think. I know William wouldn't lie to me, and neither would you."

Satisfied that his patient was calm for the time being, Uncle Cuyler sat next to Stephen again. "William and I often disagree. It has been that way for several years—ever since the Stamp Act. But I respect William."

"You do?"

"Yes, and you should, too."

"But if you don't agree with him, how can you respect him?"

"William is a man who thinks for himself. And that is what I respect. He does what he believes is right before God. He is a man of integrity."

"But what if what William thinks is right really is wrong?"

Cuyler raised his eyes to the cot across the room and pondered the question. "No matter what any of us thinks, we all have to face that question. If a deadly deed is done in the name of patriotism or loyalty, is it noble? If a good deed is done out of fear, does it lack all virtue?"

"I'm not sure I understand, Uncle Cuyler."

"I'm not sure I do either, Stephen. But this is my point: You can listen to me, you can listen to William, and you can even listen to Lydia. But in the end, you must find your own answers. And only God can give you the answers."

"But you and William both believe in God. You both go to church; you both pray. Why doesn't God tell you the same thing?"

Cuyler nodded. "That is one of the great mysteries of our time, Stephen. And I struggle with that question every day."

CHAPTER 8
The Funeral

The relentless March wind whipped through the crowd and chapped Stephen's cheeks. His nose started to run. He sniffled and tried to ignore the slow drip. He clenched his fists and pulled them up into his coat sleeves to keep them from the cold, raw air. Stephen stood with his parents and his sisters on the side of King Street, watching but not participating in what was happening. Uncle Ethan, back from New York at last, was with them.

Three days had passed since the shooting in King Street. William had hardly been home at all during those three days. Stephen went to bed in their room alone, and when he woke, William's bed would be rumpled but empty.

The streets had been strangely quiet, even during the hours when merchants usually did most of their business. Governor Hutchinson, who had finally dispersed the crowd on the night of the shooting, stayed hidden from sight much of the time. Sam Adams, however, walked the streets with the Sons of Liberty.

Stephen's sister Kathleen had said that Samuel Adams looked like he had worn his clothes to bed every night for a week. His wig was never on straight, and he seemed to have trouble keeping a job. Often he did not know where his next meal was coming from. Still, he committed himself to the one cause he believed in: overthrowing British oppression. He wrote so many letters to the newspapers in Boston that Richard Lankford would groan aloud when he saw the handwriting that had become familiar to every editor in town.

After the shootings, Sam Adams made no threats and gave no hints that he was planning any action that would stir up the people more. Yet Governor Hutchinson and the other British officials watched him carefully. Even when he seemed to be doing nothing, Sam Adams could make people think he was stirring up trouble. The Sons of Liberty could fly into action at a moment's notice.

Stephen felt Kathleen's hand on his shoulder and looked up at her.

"Are you warm enough?" she asked.

Stephen shivered but nodded. He was as warm as anyone could expect to be, so he would not complain. He turned his back to the street and raised his arm to block the glare of the winter sun.

Patrick Carr was still critically ill. Uncle Cuyler and the other doctors worked to keep him stable and comfortable, but he was worse every day. Stephen had visited the clinic every day during Uncle Cuyler's shift to see for himself. Patrick's face was gray, and his breathing heavy. Every day Stephen hoped for a turnaround. But every day Patrick Carr was closer to death.

The four who had already died were to be buried today. All activity in Boston had shut down in the late afternoon. The schools remained closed. Merchants left their shops. Mothers bundled up their children against the March temperatures. Even the Lankfords had come out to watch respectfully as four caskets were carried through the streets to the cemetery.

When it was over, Papa would go back to the print shop to write a story about it for the next edition of the newspaper. It seemed to Stephen that everyone would have seen the funeral for themselves. Who would be left to read about it in the paper?

"Why can't we march?" Lydia whined. "I want to march in the funeral procession."

"It is unbecoming to make a spectacle out of the deaths of these men," Papa told his squirming daughter. He put a hand firmly on her shoulder to make sure she could go nowhere.

"But everyone else is marching. There must be five thousand people in the street."

"I would guess more like ten thousand," Papa said. "Maybe even twelve."

Sam Adams had organized the funeral. He had been quiet since the "massacre," as he called the shootings. But he was not wasting his time. The funeral was a chance for the Sons of Liberty to let the people of Boston know that everything was under control. Sam had enlisted members of the Sons of Liberty to carry the coffins ceremonially through the streets of Boston, one by one.

The route included a symbolic turn around the Liberty Tree. Whether or not the four men had belonged to the Sons of Liberty did not matter. Sam Adams presented them as a visible reminder that the British were oppressing the colonies. The elm stood solidly as a reminder to all of Boston of the zeal of Sam Adams and the Sons of Liberty. After circling the tree, the men proceeded up the hill to the burying ground.

Stephen studied the thousands of people who marched behind the coffin. He had never before seen so many people together in one place. He was curious.

"Did all these people really know the men who were killed?" Stephen asked his father. "I can't imagine having twelve thousand friends."

"That's because you're not a hero," Lydia snapped.

"Lydia!" Papa warned his daughter with his tone. To Stephen he said, "No, all these people did not know them. But they have come out of respect, as we have."

"Are they heroes, Papa?" Stephen asked.

"Some people believe they are," his father answered.

"I believe they are!" Uncle Ethan burst into the quiet conversation. "They were willing to give their lives for the freedom of Boston. I think that makes them heroes."

"We're not at all sure that is what happened," Papa said. "Cuyler and dozens of other men tell a different story."

"Cuyler is becoming more of a Loyalist every day," Uncle Ethan said. "His perspective on the facts is colored by his leanings."

"Don't you think your Patriot leanings influence your perspective?" Papa challenged.

"Please," Mama pleaded, "let's not have an argument standing out on a street corner during a funeral."

Her husband and her brother quieted, and they all continued watching. The funeral procession plodded past them with the second casket. The six men who carried it on their shoulders, dressed in their finest black clothes, wore somber expressions and looked only ahead of them. Behind them came several thousand mourners. Some were sincere; others were there out of curiosity. The crowd buzzed with opinions and comments. Stephen turned his head from one conversation to another.

"We will always remember the Boston Massacre, and it will

strengthen us to defy the British so that these men did not die in vain."

"We must not allow them to die for nothing."

Stephen pondered the phrase "Boston Massacre." That sounded like the troops had killed the men on purpose. But had they? Another fragment of conversation drifted toward him.

"Crispus Attucks was black. Can he still be a hero?"

"Any man who gives his life for this cause is a hero."

"If only Patrick Carr were here. I'm sure he would have a few words to say to the British officials."

But Patrick Carr could not be there. Stephen wondered how many people were even thinking about Patrick Carr right now. Did they know how sick he was?

"Those soldiers should be hung as soon as possible."

"Governor Hutchinson promises that there will be a fair trial."

"Only one verdict is fair. Guilty!" The man who said this spoke gruffly and loudly and stood only a few feet away from the Lankfords. Stephen checked to see if his father was listening. Papa turned to the man and started to say something. The touch of his wife's hand on his arm held him back.

"He's right, you know," Uncle Ethan whispered. "For British troops to fire into an unarmed assembly of citizens and kill four of them is illegal and unforgivable. If we let this go by, the British can come in and massacre all of us whenever they want."

"That is not going to happen," Papa said. "We are subjects of the Crown. We have the king's protection."

"Don't be too sure of that."

"Hey, look!" Lydia shouted as she pointed at the procession. "There's William. Please, may I go walk beside William?"

"No, you may not," Mama said sharply. "You will stay exactly where you are standing."

"Mama, please."

"Mind your mother, Lydia," Papa said.

Stephen searched the procession until he had spotted his older brother. William was tall and easy to find. His brown eyes met Stephen's. William's eyes burned with belief in what he was doing. The sleepless nights he sat up writing flyers for the Sons of Liberty, the long meetings under the Liberty Tree in the middle of winter, the missed meals—William did not seem to mind any of that. It was as if he had no choice but to devote his energy to resisting British oppression.

Stephen's eyes were wide with questions about what he was watching. Why had all these people come to the funeral? The four men who died were ordinary men who would not have been known by twelve thousand people. If one of them had been struck down by a runaway horse, not more than a hundred people would have come to see him buried. Yet Papa thought there were twelve thousand people marching in the procession, and there were thousands more watching from the sidelines.

"You should be proud of William," Uncle Ethan said to Papa and Mama. "He has grown into a fine young man. I hope my own boys learn to act with as much conviction as he has."

"I want all my children to do what they know is right," Papa said.

Stephen looked into his father's eyes. He couldn't tell if Papa was really proud of William or not. But that was the way Papa was. He wanted to be fair. It did not matter if people could tell what he was thinking. Papa did not always agree with what William did.

Was he proud of him anyway? Would he ever be proud of Stephen?

William moved down the street and was lost in the crowd again. The third coffin was coming into view from the other direction. When the funeral had begun late that March afternoon, no one had known how ·many people would come to pay their respects. But after watching and listening, Stephen decided that most of the people had come to pay their respects to the Patriots' cause, not to the four men who were being buried. He felt sad about that.

"Ethan," Mama said, as they were waiting for the next coffin to pass them, "have you and Dancy given that child a name yet?"

Uncle Ethan laughed. "I'm afraid we can't seem to agree on anything except that she is a beautiful little creature."

"I don't understand why the task is so difficult."

"I only got home yesterday," Uncle Ethan reminded his sister. "We have not really had time to discuss names."

"Is the baby all right?" Stephen asked. He knew from talking to Uncle Cuyler how many babies died within a few weeks after being born. Several of his friends had lost little brothers or sisters. He shivered in the March chill and thought of the tiny baby being held in her mother's arms at home next to the warm fire.

"The child is fine," Uncle Ethan said confidently. "She is so small that I can almost hold her in one hand. But her cry is every bit as loud and demanding as the boys' when they were babies."

Mama laughed. Stephen felt better. How badly he wanted the baby to thrive and grow strong. If only he could protect her from the sorrow of the night of her birth.

The fourth casket came into view. Stephen did not want to watch anymore.

CHAPTER 9

Important News

"Stephen! Over here!"

Stephen blinked into the bright sunlight outside the school-house a few days later. William was waiting for him with the horse and cart that he used for delivering newspapers in the afternoon.

"What are you doing here?" Stephen asked. He walked toward William, glancing over his shoulder for Lydia. His usual afternoon routine was to wait for Lydia, who liked to dillydally after school, and the two of them would walk home together. Sometimes they would stop by their father's print shop.

"Where's Lydia?" Will asked. His eyes scanned the school yard. He was in a hurry.

"She's still inside," Stephen said. "She likes to talk to her friends after school. What's happening?"

"She doesn't have time for gossiping today," Will said. "We've got to get going."

"Why? What's going on?" Will was not answering his questions, and Stephen was getting more anxious by the moment.

"Go back in and get Lydia," Will said, "and tell her to hurry."

"William! Tell me what's happening. Is Mama all right? Papa?"

Lydia appeared in the doorway. At the sight of William, she

forgot all about her friends and dashed toward him.

"William!" Stephen was certain his sister's screech could be heard for blocks.

"Quickly, get in the cart. Both of you." William gestured that they should hurry.

"You mean we don't have to walk home today?" Lydia clambered up into the seat in front of the cart, while Stephen jumped into the open back. William took the reins and immediately started the horse in a quick trot.

"William, you're scaring me," Stephen called from the back.

"I'm sorry, Stephen. Everybody is fine. No one is ill."

"Then why have you come for us?" The cart rumbled along. Stephen held tight to the side to keep from falling over.

"While you were in school today, the grand jury met."

"What does that mean?"

"It means that Captain Preston and eight soldiers will stand trial for the massacre last week. The prosecuting attorney believes he has enough evidence to convict them of murder."

"Oh," Stephen said, and he leaned back against the side of the cart.

Lydia was thrilled with the news. "This is what you wanted, isn't it, William?"

"It's the first step toward justice," William said. He slapped the mare's rump to make her go even faster.

"I still don't understand," Stephen said. "Why would you come all the way over to the school to tell us that?"

"I need the two of you to do the deliveries this afternoon."

Lydia groaned. "I hate delivering newspapers. They're so dirty and heavy. And they smell funny."

"That's the ink," Stephen said matter-of-factly.

"You can do this," William said. "Kathleen and I used to do this when we were your age. Use the map that I drew for you a few months ago. This is the kind of emergency the map is for. I marked an X on all the corners where you need to leave papers."

"But where will you be?" Lydia asked.

"I have some important business to take care of."

Lydia's eyes widened with excitement. "Sons of Liberty business?"

"Never mind what the business is. Just deliver the papers."

They pulled up in front of the print shop. William jumped down and flew through the door. Stephen and Lydia followed him in.

"Papa, Stephen and Lydia are here." He stopped abruptly. "Oh, hello, Uncle Cuyler."

"Hello, William."

Stephen furrowed his brow thoughtfully. William and Uncle Cuyler had become very cool toward one another in the last few days.

Papa set a jumbled tray of metal letters on the counter and began putting them back in their proper places. "Uncle Cuyler just heard the news about the grand jury," he said. "He wanted to read our story."

"I'm glad to see that the course of justice will be followed," Uncle Cuyler said to William. "I heard some rumors that the Sons of Liberty were threatening to take matters into their own hands."

"We all want justice," William said. He took a rag from the counter and wiped the press in random places. "It's only a matter of time before those men will hang."

"I'm disappointed to hear you say that," Uncle Cuyler said. "I was hoping you would have an open mind toward justice. The men have not yet been tried. How can you know they deserve to hang?"

"Under the law, hanging is the penalty for murder."

"True enough—but only men who have committed murder deserve the penalty."

"The jury will confirm what we already know."

"I trust that your own personal opinions will not influence your work on the paper," Uncle Cuyler said evenly.

"My father does not complain about my work." William locked his eyes onto his uncle's.

"Nor should he." Uncle Cuyler met William's gaze evenly. "He has a reputation for being fair-minded. I'm sure you appreciate the importance of that quality in Boston right now. I know you would do nothing to compromise your father's reputation."

Stephen suddenly realized he had been holding his breath while he listened to this exchange between his brother and his uncle. He gasped for air.

William turned to Stephen. "I'll help you load the papers. Then I have to go."

"I don't want to deliver papers," protested Lydia. "I want to go with William."

"You will do as you are told," Papa said. "We tied the papers in smaller bundles so you will have no difficulty lifting them."

Lydia groaned, but she returned to the cart. "At least I get to drive the cart. Stephen is much too young for that!"

"Slow down!" Stephen called from the back of the cart. "You're going past the marks on the map."

Lydia yanked on the reins and brought the cart to an awkward stop. Stephen slammed into the side of the cart. She looked at him with eyes full of mischief. "Is that slow enough for you?"

Stephen sighed, then jumped off the back of the cart and ran with a bundle of papers to the shop they had passed. Word had already spread around town about the indictments. People were eager to see the paper.

"It won't be long now," the merchant said as he scanned the headline. "We'll have us a public hanging of nine lobsterbacks."

"That will teach the rest of them not to push around the people of Boston," a customer added.

Stephen walked back to the cart, wondering why everyone— except Uncle Cuyler—was so sure the men would be found guilty.

"Did you hear? Did you hear?" a schoolmate ran alongside Stephen the next afternoon. Stephen had been walking very slowly, hoping that Lydia would soon realize how late it was getting and leave her friends so they could go home.

"About the indictments?" Stephen answered his schoolmate. "Of course I heard. My father publishes a newspaper."

"No, not that. That's yesterday's news."

"What are you talking about?"

"Patrick Carr. He died today."

Stephen hardly glanced over his shoulder at Lydia. It took him only a fraction of a second to decide what he would do. Without another word to his friend or a thought about Lydia, he sped off toward Uncle Cuyler's clinic. Yesterday Patrick had opened his eyes for a few minutes while Stephen visited. Stephen had wanted very much to believe that this was a good sign. And now the news of his death!

As he ran through the commons, past the Customs House, and down King Street, he saw people talking in little groups. Even though he did not stop, portions of their conversations wafted to his ears.

"The British will pay for this!"

"Patrick Carr's death will be added to the indictments! He was murdered just as surely as the others."

"We will have our revenge when those men hang!"

"Tomorrow would not be soon enough for me."

Stephen burst breathless through the doors of Uncle Cuyler's clinic.

"Is it true? Is he. . . ?" He looked toward the cot. It was empty and freshly made up. "I thought he was better. Yesterday he looked at me."

"He was very badly wounded, Stephen. You knew that." Uncle Cuyler caught his nephew up in a hug. "We did everything we could for him. It wasn't enough."

"Were you here?"

"No. Dr. Jeffries was with him."

"Now everyone wants the soldiers to be tried for murdering Patrick Carr, too. I heard people talking in the streets."

"Yes, I know. I expected that." Uncle Cuyler led Stephen to a chair.

"The Sons of Liberty will have another funeral, and everyone will come and watch. They'll say horrible things about the British soldiers all over again."

Uncle Cuyler nodded. "But Dr. Jeffries told me something interesting about Patrick Carr's last moments."

"What was that?"

"Patrick said that he bore the soldiers no malice."

Stephen was puzzled. "What does that mean?"

Uncle Cuyler leaned back in his chair and spoke thoughtfully. "I think Patrick knew that the soldiers were in a difficult situation and responded as any of us would. He did not hold their actions against them."

"So it is not their fault?"

"Patrick Carr did not think so."

"But everyone else in Boston does."

"Not everyone."

"Everyone except you."

Uncle Cuyler shook his head adamantly. "I am not alone in my opinion. Those of us who disagree with the Sons of Liberty are not as visible as they are. But we have great confidence that the justice system will treat these men properly."

"Will Dr. Jeffries tell the judge what Patrick said? Will it make a difference?"

Uncle Cuyler shrugged. "The decision will be in the hands of the jury." He looked at Stephen with raised eyebrows. "Does your father know you are here?"

Stephen shook his head. "I came straight from school. Lydia's going to be really mad, too. I didn't wait for her."

"Come on. I'll walk you over to the print shop, and we'll make sure everything is all right."

Stephen was right. Lydia was annoyed that Stephen had left her to walk alone. But his father was simply relieved that Stephen was safe. His older sister Kathleen was there too, working on typesetting some flyers.

"Where is William?" Stephen asked.

"With the Sons of Liberty, of course," Lydia said. "Where would you expect him to be on a day like this?"

"What about the papers? Is he coming to deliver them?"

Papa shrugged. "If he does not get here in a few minutes, you and Lydia will have to do it again."

Lydia moaned.

The print shop door opened, and in came William.

"Just in time!" Lydia said gleefully.

"We've done it!" William announced. "We have beaten the British."

"William!" Uncle Cuyler said harshly. "Another man died today. I hardly think that is cause for rejoicing."

"No, of course not." William sobered for a moment. "I'm as sorry about Patrick Carr as you are, Uncle Cuyler. That's not what I'm talking about."

With puzzled eyes, everyone looked at William.

"The troops are being withdrawn," William announced.

"The troops are being withdrawn?" his father echoed.

"Yippee!" shouted Lydia. She threw a stack of flyers into the air.

Stephen glanced at Uncle Cuyler for his response.

"When?" Uncle Cuyler asked quietly.

"Immediately." The sound of victory in William's voice was unmistakable. "This is the beginning of the end of British oppression."

Kathleen leaned across the counter. "How do you know the troops won't be back when Boston has quieted down?" she asked.

William shrugged carelessly. "We won't let them back this time. We are much more organized than we were two years ago when they first arrived in such numbers. Sam Adams has a wide following—and not just in the Sons of Liberty. We simply would not allow them to row ashore."

"Britain has a much larger army than Boston can muster," Uncle Cuyler said.

"But don't you see, Uncle Cuyler? It's not just Boston. It's all the colonies. Ever since the Stamp Act, leaders in all the colonies have been thinking alike. The British are only beginning to realize what they are up against."

"The British Parliament is a powerful institution, William. It will not be as easy as you think."

"The Patriots are quite serious, Uncle Cuyler. Do not take us lightly."

Kathleen turned back to her typesetting. Papa took the rag from William and continued wiping off the press.

"I'd better get back to the clinic," Uncle Cuyler said. He stepped toward the door.

"I'll get the cart loaded," William mumbled. "Then I have to leave."

Stephen watched as everyone turned back to the work that gave structure to their days in times of great change.

Was William right? Was this really the beginning of the end?

CHAPTER 10

Family Feud

Captain Preston and the other twelve men accused of crimes were jailed.

Stephen had seen the inside of the jail once. What he remembered most about it were the strong walls. There was one tiny window high in the wall with bars across the glass. A bundle of straw served as the bed. The heavy wooden door had a slot in it, through which the prisoner received his food. If the prisoner had any energy for resisting imprisonment, he was put in iron chains. Jail was a dismal place.

Stephen thought of Thomas Preston, captain in the king's army, wearing his fine red coat. Thinking of a man like that sitting in a dark cell on a damp pile of straw was an ugly picture. Whenever it came into Stephen's mind, he blinked his eyes until it went away.

Despite the ugliness of prison, Uncle Cuyler thought it was the safest place for the accused men to be. Many people in Boston were ready to take the law into their own hands and hang the men at the first chance they got. If the men were walking around free, their lives would be in danger, and a jury would never get the chance to decide their guilt or innocence. If justice was to be served, Uncle Cuyler kept saying, the men should stay in prison until their innocence was proven. Even then it might not be safe for them to walk the streets.

Boston thrived under the management of Sam Adams and the Sons of Liberty. The thousands of British troops were gone, and Boston felt freer than it had for years. Technically, the governor and officials appointed by Parliament were in charge, but anyone who lived in Boston knew that it was the Sons of Liberty who were running the city.

More and more often, William recruited Stephen and Lydia to deliver papers because he had other things to do—things that he felt were of utmost importance. With the soldiers gone, Bostonians were left to quarrel among themselves. It was becoming more and more difficult to remain neutral on political questions. To be a Loyalist meant to support the king and Parliament and accept their right to govern the colonies any way they saw fit. On the other hand, to be a Patriot meant to detest anything British and do everything possible to throw out the British. There was very little ground in between the two extremes.

William and Uncle Cuyler had learned to hold their tongues with each other—most of the time. Uncle Ethan just shook his head at the path his younger brother had chosen. Stephen hated to see squabbling in the family.

The trials of the accused men did not happen as quickly as everyone expected. The judge who was to preside over the case became ill, and Preston and the others needed time to find lawyers who were willing to defend them. Spring stretched into early summer as the men languished in their cells and all of Boston waited for justice.

Stephen was enjoying a new sense of freedom. School was not in session in June, and the troops were gone. He could walk from home to the print shop or Uncle Cuyler's clinic whenever he wanted.

When he arrived at the print shop one afternoon in late June, Stephen's heart sank. As soon as he pushed open the door, he could hear William's raised voice. His whole family was there. Kathleen had come in to work on a typesetting project, Lydia had been tagging along after William every chance she got, and Mama had just brought a basket of lunch. When Stephen arrived, the Lankford family was all in one place—but not exactly enjoying one another's company.

"Papa, you cannot possibly print this!" William was red-faced and serious.

"I have an obligation to my readers." Papa dampened the paper in the press, preparing to print on it.

"Have you no sense of patriotism, Papa?" William had lowered his voice, but he had not changed his tone.

Richard Lankford glared at his oldest son until William shamefully turned his eyes to the floor.

Stephen had no idea what they were talking about, but it must have been very serious to make William speak to his father in such a tone. Circling around the edge of the room, Stephen decided he would ask Kathleen what the argument was about.

"If you feel this work is beyond your conscience, you may be excused for the afternoon," Papa said. He straightened the paper in the tray. "I am not a member of the Sons of Liberty. Sam Adams has not earned my undivided, unthinking loyalty."

"My loyalty is not unthinking," William retorted. "My loyalty to Sam comes from a deep conviction that he is the leader who will bring fairness and freedom to the colonies. I am honored to be associated with him."

Stephen reached Kathleen and tugged on her sleeve. "What are they fighting about?" he asked quietly.

Kathleen set down a tray of letters and sighed. "Captain Preston wrote a letter to the king. Papa wants to print it, and William does not think he should."

"Why not?"

"Because Captain Preston is defending himself in the letter."

"If he didn't think he did anything wrong, why shouldn't he defend himself?"

"William thinks Captain Preston went too far. In the letter, he did not just defend himself. He almost came right out and accused several men of starting a fight with the sentry that night on purpose. William does not want Papa to print that part of the letter."

"Captain Preston really does think somebody planned the massacre?"

"Not exactly. Captain Preston believes that there was a group of men determined to break into the Customs House and steal money."

"The Customs House is where they put the money for the king."

"Right," Kathleen said. "Captain Preston said the men wanted to take that money back. If they would have to kill the sentry on duty to get into the building, then they were willing to do that."

"Ow!" Stephen wheeled around to see that Lydia had snuck up on him and poked him in the back. "Stop that, Lydia."

"Oh, don't be such a baby."

"I'm not a baby."

"Maybe not, but you're a Loyalist, aren't you?"

"Don't be silly," Kathleen said. "Stephen is far too young to get involved on either side of a political question—as are you."

Lydia stamped her foot. "I'm old enough to think for myself, and I agree with William. Papa should not let the paper be used to defend Captain Preston's outrageous order to fire on an innocent crowd."

"It's Papa's job as owner of the newspaper to keep people informed. This is news. Everyone will be interested in the letter whether they agree with it or not."

Stephen nodded his emphatic agreement with what Kathleen had said. Lydia rolled her eyes.

At the sound of a chair scraping across the floor, they turned their attention back to William and their father. William sat heavily in the wooden chair.

"If you have any respect for me at all, you will not print that letter," William said.

"William, you will gain nothing by putting me in a difficult position. Your mother and I have raised you well. You know what you believe, and you have the courage to act on your convictions. You must allow me to do the same." Papa raised his eyes to Kathleen. "We don't have time for a rest, Kathleen. Keep working on the type."

Kathleen's hands flew into action again. Stephen could see the letter she was copying from. It had already been printed in the newspapers in England and read by the king and the members of Parliament. Only recently had a ship brought a copy of it back across the ocean to the city where the letter had been written weeks ago.

William was silent. Papa continued preparing the press. Stephen held his breath, waiting to see what William would say next. At last William spoke.

"At least let Sam Adams write a companion article. He spoke to Preston and challenged the contents of the letter. Preston did not deny that someone may have tampered with his words."

"There is no time for that today. We must begin printing in the next few minutes."

"Please, take time for a bit of lunch." Mama had spread a cloth across the counter and laid out bread, cheese, and coffee.

"What about tomorrow?" William pressed his father further, without responding to the invitation to lunch. "We could print Sam's article tomorrow. Give him a chance to get to the truth behind Preston's accusations."

Papa paused to consider William's proposal. "The article must be on my desk first thing in the morning."

"That is fair."

"And I reserve the right to approve it before we print."

"I understand."

"So be it." Papa turned to Kathleen. "Is the first page of type almost ready?"

"Yes, Papa, just a few more words."

"Richard, please, eat some lunch." Mama gestured again to the lunch. "Children, come and eat. There is plenty for all of you."

William stood up, walked over to his mother, and kissed her cheek. "I'm sorry, Mama. The lunch looks lovely. But I have no time to eat it now."

"Will you be home for supper?"

"I'm not sure. Don't wait for me."

"Can I come with you?" Lydia linked her arm through William's.

Mama threw a sharp look at Lydia. "You know the answer to that."

William released his arm from Lydia's hold. "We'll talk about all this later."

William left then, and Lydia scowled. Papa and Kathleen went back to work. Stephen watched his mother nibble at a piece of bread. Her face was drawn and her shoulders rigid.

Stephen stepped up to the counter. "I would like some lunch, Mama."

Mama smiled through her strain at her youngest child. "Have as much as you like, Stephen. It appears that I brought more than we need." She glanced hopefully at her husband. He glanced back, but he made no move to come and eat.

"Lydia, come and eat," Mama said.

Lydia had her face pressed against the window in the front of the shop, watching William disappear from sight.

"He went to the Liberty Tree," she said. "I just know that's where he went."

"Pay no mind to William's whereabouts," Mama said. "Come and eat."

"I'm not hungry."

"You must eat properly, or you'll fall ill."

"I'm not hungry!" Lydia insisted, not moving from the window.

"Do as your mother says," Papa commanded. But he did not stop working.

Dragging her feet noisily, Lydia crossed over to the counter and picked up a piece of cheese. "Kathleen," she said, "William told me that when you were my age you actually wanted to help a British soldier."

Stephen stopped chewing and looked up at Kathleen. A wave of pain crossed her face before she answered. He forced the lump in his throat down. Kathleen spoke calmly, but her voice quivered ever so slightly.

"That's right, Lydia. I did. He was hungry and cold. He had been shot during a Stamp Act riot. I helped Uncle Cuyler nurse him back to health. I'm only sorry that I could not have done more for him."

"But he was a British soldier!" Lydia protested with disgust.

"He was a human being," Kathleen said simply. "He died a few months later. He was only sixteen." She turned away to put the last letter of type in place.

"You and Stephen are just alike." Lydia tossed her unmanageable hair over her shoulder and picked up a piece of cheese. "You sympathize with the British so much that you are almost lobsterbacks yourselves. It's because you spend too much time with Uncle Cuyler."

"Lydia, hold your tongue!" Papa's voice meant what he said.

Stephen threw down a half-eaten piece of bread and wheeled around at Lydia.

"And you are too much like William!" he shouted. "Nothing matters to you except the Patriot cause."

"It is the most important thing!" Lydia retorted.

"What about truth?" Stephen challenged. "Doesn't that matter?"

Stephen ran to the door and yanked it open. Both his parents were calling to him, but he ignored them and ran out into the street. He had to get away from Lydia.

CHAPTER 11
Escape

Stephen tumbled out into the street, hardly able to see through the tears welling up in his eyes. He heard the print shop door open behind him and his mother's voice pleading for him to come back. But he did not want to face her just then. He did not want to see the lines in her face that deepened with every political quarrel that erupted in the family.

It was bad enough that her two brothers, Uncle Ethan and Uncle Cuyler, held opposing views. And even though Papa and William agreed on many things, they quarreled about the best way to bring change to the colonies. Lydia never missed a chance to side with William, no matter whose feelings she hurt. Stephen was tired of it all. So he kept running.

He kicked at the cobblestones with his boot. All he accomplished was to hurt his toe. With the back of his hand, he wiped the tears from his eyes. He was hurt by the spiteful way Lydia spoke to him. But even more than that, he was angry at himself for letting her upset him.

His feet took him where they most naturally wanted to go—across the town square to Uncle Cuyler's medical clinic. Whenever he needed refuge, he went to the clinic. The building itself, with its warm wood tones, comforted him. The clinic was a place where anyone could come for help, Patriot or Loyalist. Uncle Cuyler had worked hard to make sure the clinic was neutral territory, no matter what his own political opinions were.

And if his uncle was there, Stephen knew that he could stay as long as he liked. He only had to stay out of the way while Uncle Cuyler was with a patient. Sometimes Anna was there, too. Anna had told him she would be there all that morning. It was barely lunchtime. Stephen hoped she would still be there.

As he rounded the last corner, Stephen forced himself to slow down and catch his breath. He made sure his cheeks were dry of tears. Anna and Uncle Cuyler were sitting on a bench in front of the clinic munching on lunch. Uncle Cuyler was leaning back comfortably with his long legs stretched out in front of him, crossed at the ankles. Anna swung her short legs in the wide space beneath the bench. They looked content to be together.

Stephen smiled weakly at them.

"Do you feel all right, Stephen?" Uncle Cuyler asked. "You look a little red in the face."

"I'm all right," Stephen said. "I've just been running—that's all." He hoped that they would not be able to tell he had been crying—almost.

"What is the hurry?" Anna asked.

Stephen shrugged. How could he explain the scene that had driven him from the print shop?

"Have you had lunch?" Uncle Cuyler asked. He offered Stephen a piece of dried meat.

Stephen thought of the half-eaten chunk of bread he had left on his father's counter. He felt guilty about running out on his mother's lunch. She would ask him later if he had eaten anything.

Stephen accepted the meat. "Thanks," he said. With the knot in his stomach, he did not know if there would be any space for food.

Anna scooted over. "There's room for you here."

Stephen squeezed in between Anna and Uncle Cuyler. He felt calmer immediately. Settling back against the bench, he looked absently out into the street, in the direction he had just come from. He wondered why was it so easy for him to be with Uncle Cuyler and Anna.

"I saw your mother carrying a basket to the print shop awhile ago," Uncle Cuyler said.

"I know." Stephen nibbled politely on the meat.

"You are welcome to share our lunch," Uncle Cuyler said. "But if you are still hungry, I'm sure your mother has plenty."

"I know. I was just there."

"Oh?" Uncle Cuyler raised an eyebrow and questioned Stephen with his eyes.

Stephen looked away. If he confided in Uncle Cuyler, he would have to repeat what Lydia had said. And he did not want to hurt Uncle Cuyler. He did not want Uncle Cuyler to know Lydia had said something mean about him. He did not want to explain why he was there and not at the print shop eating lunch with his own family.

The three sat in silence for several minutes. Anna crunched on a carrot. Uncle Cuyler uncrossed his long legs and stretched one arm across the back of the bench. Stephen tried to swallow a bite, but he was having a hard time.

Uncle Cuyler scanned the sky. Occasional fluffs of white

drifted across the peaceful blue expanse. "Looks like a good day for fishing, don't you think?"

"I suppose so," Stephen agreed reluctantly. He had not really noticed the weather before that point in the day.

"Can we go? Can we go?" Anna loved to fish.

"I'll tell you what," Uncle Cuyler said. "I have to stay here and see patients this afternoon. But I don't see why you two shouldn't go. I happen to have two poles propped up behind my office door. And the widow Spencer said we could fish in the pond at the back of her property on any day of our choosing."

"Let's do it, Stephen!" Anna cried.

"Can we go alone?" Stephen asked. He was still not used to the freedom of Boston without British troops, and he'd always thought the widow Spencer was a scary person.

"I don't see why not. It's not very far away."

"I don't know." Stephen seemed hesitant.

"Don't worry about your folks," Uncle Cuyler said. "I'll send a message about where you are."

"Come on, Stephen; it'll be fun!"

Anna's enthusiasm won him over. "All right, I'd like to go fishing."

They packed up the rest of the lunch, slung Uncle Cuyler's poles over their shoulders, and headed for the widow Spencer's property. They left the cobblestones of downtown Boston and followed the dirt road that led to the outskirts of town.

"All right, Stephen," Anna said, "we're alone now, so you can tell me what is bothering you."

Stephen smiled at his cousin gratefully.

"It's Lydia, isn't it?" Anna said.

"How did you know?" Somehow Anna always knew what he was thinking.

"Because she is the only person who bothers you so."

Stephen kicked a loose rock in the dirt. "She makes me angry. I get frustrated with the way she talks about the British. She thinks the British do everything wrong and the Sons of Liberty do everything right."

"You pay too much attention to Lydia," Anna said. "You should not let her bother you."

"That's easy for you to say. But she's my sister. She lives in the same house. And my parents think we should do everything together."

"And she likes to talk," added Anna.

Stephen laughed. "Yes, most of all, she likes to talk."

"She just says the things she hears. She doesn't really understand everything she hears. Lots of people in Boston are that way. That's what my father says."

"Lydia doesn't care what your father says." Stephen shifted his fishing pole to the other shoulder.

"Well, she ought to care. My parents are Loyalists. Uncle Ethan and Aunt Dancy are Patriots. So is William. But we're all in the same family."

"Deep down, my parents are Patriots, too," Stephen said.

"But they all want the same thing," Anna insisted.

"No, they don't," objected Stephen. "Your parents want the colonies to be part of England, and William and Uncle Ethan think the colonies are ready to be a separate country."

"But don't you see? They all want what they think is best for the colonies."

"But they don't agree on what is best." Stephen kicked at the ground in frustration. Dry dirt sprayed up in front of them.

"That's not the important part," Anna said. "What matters is that everyone wants what is good for Boston and all the colonies."

"That's the part that Lydia forgets."

"And that's why you have to remember it."

Stephen did not respond. What Anna said made sense. But how was that going to help him get along with Lydia?

They arrived at the widow Spencer's pond and cast their lines. To Stephen's relief, the widow was nowhere to be seen. Anna took off her socks and shoes and wiggled her toes into the dirt. Giggling, Stephen did the same. The damp black earth at the edge of the pond oozed between his toes. He squished his feet down deeper. It felt cool.

"Do you think this dirt was ever part of England?" Anna asked.

"What do you mean?" Stephen looked at the ground. It was ordinary dirt.

"We're on one side of the ocean, and England is on the other side. The tide washes back and forth on both sides. Maybe this very dirt used to be on the shores of England."

Stephen tilted his head. "I suppose that's possible. But it's Boston dirt now."

"That's what the Patriots would say," Anna observed.

"And the Loyalists would say that if this dirt was ever part of England, it still is."

They laughed at the strange comparison.

Anna pulled in her line and cast it out farther. "Do you think Aunt Dancy and Uncle Ethan are ever going to name their baby?"

Stephen laughed. The baby was more than three months old, and still she had no name. Aunt Dancy and Uncle Ethan's inability to agree on a name had become a family joke. Various members of the family made suggestions, which Uncle Ethan and Aunt Dancy promised to consider. But the longer the process went on, the more ridiculous the suggestions became.

"They could call her Indecisive," Anna suggested.

"Or Patience, because she waited so long for a name."

"Or Hope, because she has to hope she'll have a name someday."

"Or Tiny, because she is so small."

"Or Wakeful, because she won't sleep through the night."

"Or Quarrel, because Uncle Ethan and Aunt Dancy quarrel about her name."

Stephen dropped his pole and plopped back in the grass laughing. "Can you imagine such a name!"

"Right now they just call her Sister. I'm afraid they might decide to stay with that."

"That would be awful—not to have a real name of her own."

"Maybe we'll have to choose a name and sneak her off to the minister to be christened," Anna said, giggling.

"We'll have to try to look very tall to make him think we are the parents."

"I'll use stilts and wear one of my mother's longest dresses."

Stephen laughed at the mental image of Anna on stilts in an oversized dress.

"I just want the baby to grow up happy and to have a good life no matter what happens to Massachusetts."

After that, they did not speak. The fish were not biting, but they sat with their poles stuck in the ground and watched the pond anyway.

Stephen was glad he had escaped with Anna for the afternoon. When the two of them were together, they were just Stephen and Anna, ten-year-old cousins who enjoyed being together. They were neither British nor American, neither Loyalist nor Patriot. Just Stephen and Anna. And he liked that feeling.

Stephen stared at the pond and tossed an occasional pebble. He watched as even the tiniest pebble disturbed the smoothness of the pond. From one shore to the other, the entire pond rippled from the gentle plink of each pebble. Stephen picked up a handful of pebbles and some larger stones. He threw them in the pond, one after the other, rapidly. One ripple followed closely after the one before it.

As Stephen watched the ripples and the small waves he had created, he saw a collage of images. He saw the strain in his mother's face as she tried to keep the family together in a time of turmoil. He saw Kathleen's guarded expression as she gave the factual answers to his questions. He saw his father's determination to be fair at all times. Lydia's face rose in his mind with self-assured green eyes, and William's face burned with the fire of change. The only face missing in Stephen's mind was his own. He could not see himself, could not make out his features in the greenish background of the pond. Why wasn't he in the picture?

CHAPTER 12

The Trial

Stephen went fishing with Anna many times that summer. The Lankfords and the Turners feasted when they caught something, and their mothers were happy to have them bring home something that the British could not tax.

But it did not really matter if they caught any fish or not. They simply loved walking down the dirt road together, confiding their secrets to each other, and wading in the pond on the hottest days to cool themselves. They stretched out on the grassy slope beside the pond and daydreamed about a time when Boston would be at rest. The British troops would stay away, and Boston's citizens would stop quarreling.

The widow Spencer was not nearly as scary as Stephen had thought. It turned out that she was only sad, not mean. Mr. Spencer had been killed accidentally when Stephen and Anna were little. He had been at the wrong place at the wrong time when a street riot broke out during the Stamp Act. The Spencers did not have very strong political opinions. He was not a part of the riot. But he got knocked over, hit his head on a post, and died the next day.

The widow Spencer had never gotten over feeling angry and frustrated that her innocent husband had died for someone else's cause. She hardly talked to anyone anymore. She had stopped going to church, and she never chatted with people in the town commons. But she did seem to enjoy having Stephen and Anna come to fish. Sometimes she even brought them a snack or a cold drink.

During the summer, Boston grew restless for the trials to take place. The citizens waited impatiently for the presiding judge to regain his health, and they stormed through the streets when they heard that John Adams had agreed to defend Thomas Preston. Only two lawyers in Boston were not afraid to defend the British soldiers. Josiah Quincy Jr. was eager to assist John Adams. All of Boston respected John Adams.

Stephen remembered how surprised William was that John Adams, a distant cousin of Sam's, would take the case. John had always supported the views of the Patriots when they opposed the British. He was well known as a person who defended the rights of people living in American colonies. He believed England had been wrong to send thousands of troops to Boston. For all these ideas, William admired John Adams. But John Adams also believed that any person living in the colonies deserved a fair trial and a strong defense. So he took the case, and with the help of Josiah Quincy Jr., he put together the best defense possible.

Captain Preston's trial date kept getting pushed back later and later, until finally it was set for Wednesday, October 24. As the summer of 1770 gave way to autumn, and the farmers gathered their crops, and school resumed for the children, Stephen grew more and more nervous. Uncle Cuyler was confident that Captain Preston would have a fair trial and be found innocent.

William was certain Captain Preston would have a fair trial and be found guilty.

On the morning of October 24, Mama handed Lydia and Stephen their lunch buckets and made sure they were dressed warmly enough for the day. The two children set out on their usual route to school. Lydia put a book on her head to prove that she had practiced her posture well. Stephen giggled at the ridiculous sight. He was glad he was a boy and did not have to do that. Lydia marched ahead of Stephen. That was fine with him. They were supposed to stay together on the way to school. Stephen figured that as long as he could see Lydia ahead of him, they were together. They had plenty of time. They would not be late for school. He could not imagine what her hurry was that morning.

Then suddenly Lydia veered to the left, down a street that did not lead to school.

"Lydia!" Stephen started pumping his legs. His lunch bucket knocked against his knees. "Where are you going?"

Lydia did not slow down. Stephen ran faster, till he caught up with her and grabbed her elbow. The book on her head tumbled to the ground.

"Look what you did!" she cried.

"Where are you going?" Stephen demanded. "This is not the way to school."

"No, but it is the way to the courthouse."

"The courthouse!"

"You can go to school if you want to," she said, "but I'm going to the trial."

"Don't be silly, Lydia. You'll never be allowed inside the building."

"That doesn't matter. I know a good place outside, in the back of the building. If I sit under the window, I'll be able to hear what people are saying."

"Mama and Papa will be very angry," Stephen said.

"Mama and Papa do not have to know," Lydia answered, glaring at her brother with a dare in her eyes.

"Do you want me to lie for you?" Stephen could not believe what Lydia was asking of him.

"If they ask you if I went to the courthouse, then I suppose you'll have to tell the truth," Lydia conceded. "But they won't ask that question as long as they think I was in school as usual."

"Lydia, you could get in a lot of trouble."

Lydia scowled. "Is that all you ever think about—staying out of trouble? Stephen, there is more to life than obeying the rules all the time. You ought to try to be adventuresome once in a while."

"I can be adventuresome!"

"Oh, yes? Then prove it."

"What do you mean?"

"Skip school. Come to the courthouse with me."

Stephen scraped the toe of his boot around in the dirt. "I don't know, Lydia."

"Fraidycat!"

"I am not a fraidycat!"

"Then come with me."

"All right," Stephen decided. "I will."

Lydia led the way around to the back of the brick courthouse while a crowd of adults gathered in the front.

"Nobody will pay any attention to us back here," Lydia assured Stephen.

Stephen did not feel comfortable. His stomach had turned sour during the walk to the courthouse. His eyes darted around to see who might be watching them.

Lydia pointed up above their heads. "See those windows? All we have to do is figure out how to get up there, and we'll hear everything."

Stephen scowled. "I thought you had this all figured out. How are we going to get way up there?"

"Uncle Cuyler keeps saying you have a good brain," Lydia said. "Use it. Help me figure something out."

They looked around. The space behind the courthouse was littered with forgotten items.

"See that barrel over there?" Lydia said, pointing about twenty feet away. "Roll it over here."

"Why don't you roll it?"

"If I muss up my frock, Mama will know something's up."

Frowning, Stephen went to inspect the barrel. It was empty, and he easily tipped it over. He heard one of the slats splinter as it hit the ground. As he awkwardly rolled it toward Lydia, he said, "This barrel is half rotted. I don't think this is a good idea."

"It's the only idea we've got. Stand the barrel up over here, right under the window. Climb up on it."

"It might break," Stephen protested.

"It might not," Lydia countered.

Sighing, Stephen did as Lydia instructed. The barrel, frail as it was, held his weight.

"Now help me up."

Stephen squatted and linked his hands together. Lydia put one foot in his hands and grabbed the top of the barrel. As she hoisted herself up, the barrel creaked.

"Lydia, I don't think—"

The barrel gave way, and Lydia tumbled to the ground, knocking Stephen over. Lydia scrambled to her feet and began brushing the telltale dust off her dress. Stephen glanced around. No one seemed to notice them.

"Let's just forget this and go to school," Stephen said.

"You can if you want to," Lydia answered. "I'm staying here." She surveyed the rubble behind the courthouse again. "Look, there are some crates. We could stack them and climb up."

"Those crates won't even be as strong as that old barrel, and look where the barrel landed us."

"We'll figure something out." Lifting her skirt out of the dust with one hand, Lydia picked up a crate with the other and set it next to the brick wall.

"Maybe if we make a wide base," Stephen pondered. He picked up two more crates and set them next to the first one.

Soon they had a pyramid of crates that he was certain would be sturdy enough to hold them. They climbed the makeshift stairs and perched side by side on the top crate next to the window.

The window was closed.

"See if you can get the window open," Lydia directed.

Stephen rolled his eyes. But it was too late to back out now, he thought. So he shoved on the window frame. To his surprise, it lifted several inches.

"See?" Lydia said. "I told you this would be easy."

Lydia peered inside.

"What's happening?" Stephen asked.

"The attorney for the prosecution is saying something. I can't hear him very well. And he is using a bunch of big words. Why can't lawyers talk in plain language?"

"Do you think we're really going to be able to see what's going on from here?" Stephen was doubtful that all their effort would bring any reward.

"Maybe it's like studying French," Lydia said. "If we listen long enough, we'll start to understand the words."

They listened all day. Sometimes they could understand what was happening. When the witnesses were talking, they understood. It was when the lawyers spoke that it seemed like a foreign language. Stephen watched the movement of the sun carefully, and when it was time for school to be out, they scrambled down from the crates and took a direct route to the print shop.

William was in court. Stephen and Lydia offered to deliver newspapers without complaining and then went home for supper. Lydia even volunteered to set the table, which she hated to do.

Conversation around the table focused on the trial. Now Stephen and Lydia could figure out some of the missing pieces.

"That was quite an impressive line of witnesses the prosecution brought forth," William said. "One after the other, they seemed quite certain that Captain Preston gave the order to fire."

Papa broke off a piece of bread and put it in his mouth. He nodded, then said, "But I understand that John Adams has some impressive witnesses of his own. When time comes for the defense to present its case, he may be able to refute the statements given today."

"These men were eyewitnesses," William insisted. "They are men of honor."

"They are sailors," Papa said, "who are tired of being forced to remain in Boston to testify."

"I have confidence in the prosecuting attorney. He has worked hard to gather the evidence."

"You should not dismiss John Adams lightly," Papa said. "I have seen him in court before. He does not lose very often."

After supper, Lydia pulled Stephen aside. "I'm going back tomorrow. I want to hear the witnesses for the defense. Are you coming?"

Stephen hesitated for only a moment before nodding his head. It was exciting to watch the trial, even through a cracked window.

So they went back to their stack of crates the next day, and again the day after that. Stephen had stopped worrying about who might see them and easily settled into a familiar position on the crates. He was absorbed in the activities of the courtroom.

"Stephen and Lydia Lankford! Come down from there immediately!"

Stephen jerked around so hard that he almost upset the delicate balance of the crates. His mother stood below them, and he knew they were in trouble. Mama was furious.

Lydia groaned and began the climb down.

"How did you find out?" Lydia asked.

"I saw Mistress Sommers in the square this morning. Imagine my surprise," Mama said, "when she asked after your health. Her daughter mentioned last night that you had not been in school for several days."

"But, Mama," Lydia protested, "we wanted to see the trial."

"Obviously," Mama said, "but you did not have permission to miss school." She turned to Stephen. "I'm surprised at you, Stephen. This is not like you at all."

Stephen looked away. How could he face his mother? He had known better than to get involved in Lydia's scheme, but he had done so anyway.

Mama sent them straight home and upstairs to their rooms. They would have no supper that night. And the next day, Saturday, when they could have attended the trial, they were forbidden to leave the house.

CHAPTER 13
The Verdict

Saturday was a very long day, the longest that Stephen could remember. He was alone in the house with Lydia. The rest of the family had gone to the courthouse to watch the trial. The prosecution and defense were supposed to give their closing arguments that day. Then it would be up to the jury to decide if Thomas Preston was guilty or innocent of murder. Papa was prepared to spend all night at the print shop, if necessary, to publish the results of the trial.

But Lydia and Stephen were left to ramble around the house on their own, with strict instructions that they must not leave. Stephen made up his mind early in the day that no matter what Lydia said to him, he would not disobey his parents' direct instructions to stay in the house.

To his surprise, Lydia made no suggestions about sneaking out of the house. She pouted all day long, claiming that the punishment was more severe than the crime, but she made no effort to rebel. In fact, she hardly left the window. She could not see much from their front room. In the morning, it seemed that hundreds of people passed by, headed for the courthouse. After that, the streets were quiet while court was in session. Still Lydia watched the window. She wanted to see the first sign of the jury's verdict that afternoon.

But when the people finally began to stream down the street in the opposite direction, she saw no sign of victory on either side. Everyone simply made his or her way home as if this were a day like any other.

"I don't understand," she said to Stephen as they stood together in front of the window. "William was sure that the trial would end today."

"William can be wrong sometimes," Stephen commented.

"That was a mean thing to say!"

"But it's true. William is not in charge of the trial. He can't promise you when it will be over."

Even Lydia saw Stephen's logic this time. When Papa, Mama, William, and Kathleen finally came home at suppertime, they could talk of nothing else but the trial. Lydia pressed them with dozens of questions about every detail that had transpired.

"It is difficult to know what to believe," Kathleen said. "Two men swore that Captain Preston gave the order to fire, but others swore that he did not."

"He gave the order all right," William said confidently.

"I'm not so sure," Kathleen said. "I think the sentry fired first, after he had his musket knocked out of his hand. Then the others started shooting at random. I'm no soldier, but I would think that if the captain gave the order to fire, all the shots would have come at one time."

"You have a point," her father said. "That is exactly one of the points the defense is trying to make."

"It was hard to hear anything," William said. "Perhaps they did not all hear him give the order to fire at the same moment."

"My sources tell me that many people were daring the soldiers to fire, just as many of the witnesses said," Papa commented. "If the soldiers thought they heard the command and acted upon it, that does not mean that the captain actually gave the command. He cannot be held responsible for the actions of his men if they disobeyed his orders."

"Captain Preston said that the guns were not even loaded when the troops arrived," Mama said. She stoked the kitchen fire to start cooking the evening meal.

"Sam Adams believes differently," William countered. "He is positive the guns were loaded and the bayonets fixed on the ends of them. Sam has plenty of witnesses who would testify to that."

"All the testimony is over now," Mama said. "The responsibility is now on the jury."

Stephen entered the conversation. "If the testimony is finished, why did the trial not end?"

"The lawyers did not give their closing arguments," Papa explained. "The trial will break for the Sabbath, and then the jury will consider the matter on Monday."

Sunday was an even longer day than Saturday. At church, hardly anyone paid attention to the sermon. Instead, they pondered the trial and whispered their opinions discreetly in the pews. The minister preached about God's justice and rewards in the afterlife. Stephen did not think anyone cared about that. They wanted justice right now, not after they were dead.

The Sabbath was a day of rest. Mama had strict rules about observing the Sabbath. The family ate lightly and did nothing that

Mama considered to be unnecessary work. She forbade anyone to discuss the trial, which was the only thing they were all thinking about. It was difficult for Stephen to pass the time when he was not allowed to do anything but sit in the front room and read. The day dragged endlessly, and Stephen went to bed early. It was a relief to be able to get up and go to school on Monday morning.

Stephen was sharing a table with Wesley Mason and figuring sums when the word came. The jury took only a few hours to decide the fate of Captain Thomas Preston. They believed he was innocent of the charge. Students all over the classroom jumped out of their seats. Some were ecstatic. Others were furious. The teacher dismissed the class, and the students poured out of the little building to join the throngs in the streets of Boston.

"The Sons of Liberty will never stand for this!" Lydia declared. "How could twelve intelligent men come up with such a verdict?"

"Whether the Sons of Liberty like it or not," someone commented, "the jury's verdict is final."

"Sam Adams is a brilliant man—every bit as brilliant as his cousin John," Lydia insisted. "The Sons of Liberty will think of something."

Stephen knew only one place he wanted to be at such a moment. He found his cousin Anna in the schoolyard, and together they ran to Uncle Cuyler's clinic.

"Did you hear? Did you hear?" Anna burst through the door.

Uncle Cuyler cleared his throat loudly. He was behind a screen examining a patient.

"Oops." Anna giggled. "I'll get a lecture tonight!"

Stephen and Anna managed to contain their enthusiasm while

Uncle Cuyler finished the examination and dismissed the patient.

"It's wonderful news, isn't it?" Uncle Cuyler said, grinning.

Stephen could not help but agree. From the scraps of testimony he had heard through the window during the trial and the mealtime discussions with his family, he had come to the silent conclusion that Thomas Preston was not trying to hurt anyone. In fact, he was trying to make sure no one fired a gun.

"What will happen now, Papa?" Anna asked.

"I hope that the intelligent men of Boston will realize that Thomas Preston was given a fair trial. They must honor our system of justice and disgrace him no further."

Stephen was not convinced. "You think there will be more trouble, don't you, Uncle Cuyler?"

The smile faded from Uncle Cuyler's face. He sighed heavily. "I'm afraid the men of Boston are not as intelligent as I give them credit for. Yes, I think there will be trouble."

The clinic door swung open, startling them all. Uncle Ethan stood there, out of breath.

"Cuyler, I need to speak with you."

"Not now, Ethan. I'm sure you are disappointed with the verdict, but the jury has spoken. There is no need for us to quarrel about it any longer."

Ethan was shaking his head vigorously. "It's not the trial. It's the baby."

"The baby?" Stephen's alarm echoed Uncle Cuyler's.

"She's not breathing well, Cuyler. She's been sickly for a couple days."

"Why did you wait until now to call me?" Uncle Cuyler thrust his arms into his coat and snatched up his bag of medical supplies.

"Dancy thought it was no more than a bit of a chill. She did not want to disturb your Sabbath. But we can't calm the baby today. I'm afraid she's going to turn blue."

"Let me come with you," Stephen pleaded. "I was there when she was born. I want to be there to make sure she is all right."

Uncle Cuyler shook his head. "No, Stephen. Not this time. I want you both to run and find your mothers. Tell them to meet me at your aunt Dancy's house immediately."

Uncle Cuyler left. For an instant, Anna and Stephen looked at each other with wide, fearful eyes. Then they started to run in opposite directions.

Stephen burst into the print shop. Mama, Kathleen, and Lydia were all there.

"Mama, Uncle Cuyler needs you right away!"

Stephen gave his breathless explanation, and his mother flew out of the shop.

"I want the two of you to stay indoors now," Papa said sternly. "People are angry about the verdict. I've heard rumblings of trouble already. I don't want you out in it."

"Where's William?" Lydia wanted to know.

Papa shook his head and looked absently out the window. "I wish I knew, Lydia. I wish I knew."

"What about the papers?" Stephen asked.

"I'll do them myself this afternoon." He turned back to the press. Kathleen laid more paper in the tray, and Papa brought the great bar down to print the next copy.

Lydia pressed her face to the window. "It doesn't look so bad out there to me," she commented. "After all, it's not as if there are any British troops to worry about."

A crash outside the door, followed by the sound of scuffling feet, brought Papa to the window.

"Stay back!" he ordered. He looked out the window himself. "There will surely be a riot any minute now. We will all stay inside the shop until it is over. Is that understood?"

Lydia, Stephen, and Kathleen nodded mutely.

"Perhaps the riot will be brief this time," Papa said. "It's difficult to argue with the verdict of a court of law. People will come to their senses and go home for supper."

Papa went back to the press, with Kathleen helping him.

"Lydia, Stephen," he said. "The two of you can start folding the papers and bundling them up. I'll take them out when this is all over."

"Yes, sir," Lydia and Stephen both mumbled. They crouched side by side on the floor and folded the large press sheets into a size that was easier to handle.

At first they worked without speaking. More sounds of struggling came through the walls.

"Aren't you curious about what is happening out there?" Lydia whispered to Stephen.

"I know what is happening. It's a riot, just like all the others."

"I'm disappointed," Lydia said. "When you came to the courthouse with me, I thought you had finally gotten a sense of patriotism."

"I have plenty of patriotism," Stephen hissed back. "I love Boston as much as you do, maybe even more."

"Nobody loves Boston as much as I do," Lydia declared, still keeping her voice low. "If I were a boy and a little older, I would join the Sons of Liberty, just like William."

Stephen did not answer.

"You're lucky you're a boy," Lydia said. "You could go out and do something. You could fight for all the colonies. But you don't care about the colonies, do you?"

"Of course I do!"

"Then why don't you prove it?"

"What are you talking about?"

"Go and find out what's happening, who is fighting whom."

"You heard what Papa said."

Lydia scowled. "Papa understands why William does what he does. He would understand you, too. It's me he keeps an eye on."

Once again, Stephen did not answer.

"Are you afraid, Stephen? Is that it?" Lydia prodded.

"I'm not afraid." Stephen glanced over his shoulder at his father. Bent over the press making adjustments, Papa and Kathleen had their backs to Stephen and Lydia.

"He won't even hear you leave," Lydia said. "Just go out for a few minutes, find out what is going on, and come back and tell me."

Stephen's heart started to thunder. Why was he even considering this? He looked into Lydia's green eyes. They dared him to prove his fearless patriotism.

"All right, but I'm coming right back."

Folding a paper as he walked, Stephen moved across the room. Papa never turned around. Stephen put his hand on the latch. The sound of the press in action covered the creak of the hinge as he pulled the door open.

Stephen was outside.

CHAPTER 14
Unconscious!

Stephen ran to the tailor's shop, three doors down, and pressed himself against the brick wall. After a long while, he let out his breath. Was this a dream, he wondered, or had he really snuck out of the print shop on Lydia's dare?

He could not go back this soon without looking like a coward. Lydia expected him to return with some information about what was happening in the streets. He was not quite sure what she wanted to know or how he was supposed to learn anything. It was not as if he could walk up to John Adams and demand a report of the jury's discussions. But he would have to try whatever methods he could think of. When he returned to the print shop having completed his mission successfully, Lydia would have to stop accusing him of being afraid, and she would have to stop doubting his patriotism.

Stephen surveyed the street before him. Everyone seemed in a hurry. Many of the shops had closed early. Sensing that the evening might bring danger, the owners had locked the doors and headed for their homes. Even though the evening newspaper had not hit the streets yet, everyone seemed to know the verdict. Stephen's father often said that word of mouth was the fastest method of communication he had ever seen, but people needed to read a newspaper so they could hear both sides of the story.

William was no doubt disappointed by the verdict. *No,* Stephen corrected himself, *William is certain to be downright angry about the verdict, along with Sam Adams and the rest of the Sons of Liberty.* Suddenly Stephen knew what he needed to do to impress Lydia. If he could find William and take back a message to Lydia, she would never call him a mean name again. That was it! He would find William.

But where would William be? He had never shown up at the print shop after the jury's verdict was announced. He had to be somewhere with the Sons of Liberty. Stephen took stock of his location and mentally mapped a route to the Liberty Tree. He could take the back streets. He would stay out of the way of any mobs that might form spontaneously.

One advantage of Stephen's smallish size and quiet nature was that people did not always realize he was nearby. He discovered that he could walk without running down the street. If he stayed close to the buildings, he blended into the background. Anyone with a temper to vent tended to walk down the middle of the street. When he came upon a cluster of men at one corner, Stephen pretended to adjust his boot and stopped for a few minutes to listen.

"The prosecution should never have let John Adams change the charge from murder to manslaughter."

"I know most of the people on the jury, even if they aren't from Boston. They are Loyalists, I tell you. The jury was stacked with Loyalists."

"All that talk about self-defense! A soldier ought to have more control than to get spooked and fire a gun."

"That sentry's life was never in danger. The defense never proved that anyone in the crowd had a gun."

"Anybody with an ounce of common sense would have found Preston guilty. But what do you expect from a bunch of Loyalists? If they had any common sense, they wouldn't be Loyalists in the first place."

"They had their minds made up before they ever left the jurors' box. The jury did not stay out long enough to give thorough consideration to the evidence presented by the prosecution."

"The Sons of Liberty will not let this end here, I am sure of that."

The group of men moved along down the street. Stephen stood up and straightened his jacket. He had been successful at finding one piece of the puzzle. The jurors were not from Boston, and many of them were Loyalists. Or at least that is what one person said. Stephen had no idea who any of those men were or whether he could believe them. So maybe he had not discovered anything helpful after all.

Stephen continued on toward the Liberty Tree. The light was starting to fail now. In the gray haze of dusk, every shape around him took on an eeriness and shadowy quality. Twice he got disoriented in the back streets, but only briefly. Soon he came out in the center of town with a good view of the Liberty Tree.

Dozens of people were milling about the Liberty Tree, but not the sort of people he expected. He saw only ordinary citizens. Granted, they were more irate than usual, but they were ordinary citizens. There was no sign of Sam Adams, William Lankford, or any of the other Sons of Liberty.

Stephen slapped the side of his own head for his foolishness.

Why had he thought the Sons of Liberty might be meeting at a time like this? This was no time to stand around exchanging ideas under an elm tree. This was a time for action.

Darkness had fallen fully by now. Stephen was suddenly frightened. He would never be able to find William in the dark. Sneaking out of the print shop had been a stupid idea, and he had been foolish to let Lydia talk him into it. Surely his father would have missed him by now, and Stephen would have to face the consequences of his foolishness later. He looked back in the direction he had come from. The streets seemed fuller every minute. Turning around, he looked in the other direction— toward Uncle Ethan and Aunt Dancy's house. Actually, he was closer to their home than to the print shop.

Stephen's mind flashed back to the night of the massacre, the night the baby had been born almost eight months earlier. The streets had been just as full that night and tempers just as high. But somehow none of that had concerned him as he ran through the streets searching for help. All that mattered was the baby. The mission of finding help for Aunt Dancy and the baby had kept his feet pumping long after his own strength would have given out. Stephen had never taken time that night to question why so many folks were out.

Tonight was much the same. Stephen did not care about the results of Captain Preston's trial nearly as much as he cared about his baby cousin. If he was going to risk his safety for any cause, it would be for one he believed in, not one Lydia smothered him with.

Stephen made a decisive turn, quickened his step, and headed for Aunt Dancy and Uncle Ethan's house. The closer he got, the steadier his breathing became. Once he was inside, he would face a severe scolding, but he would be safe. And he would know whether the baby was all right. He was almost there.

A sudden thud against the back of his head brought darkness.

The cat was meowing. It was a loud sound, almost screeching. As Stephen listened, he realized the loud meowing was not angry. The cat was distressed. It gave a painful, mournful cry.

"What's wrong with the cat?" Stephen murmured, as his brown eyes fluttered open. Gradually, they focused on the face of Uncle Cuyler.

Uncle Cuyler furrowed his brow. "What cat?"

"Oh," said Stephen, breathing heavily, "it's the baby crying." He was lying on a pallet of quilts in front of the fire at Aunt Dancy's house. As he realized where he was, he understood what the sound was.

"Yes, she's been crying most of the evening."

"What's wrong?"

"She has a fever."

"Will she be all right?" Stephen tried to prop himself up. "Ow!" He moved his hand to where a sharp pain pierced him in the side.

"Take it easy," Uncle Cuyler said, helping him lie back. "I think you have a couple of broken ribs."

"The baby. . . Is she all right?"

"It's been a long night, but yes, I think she will improve."

Stephen breathed a sigh of relief. "I'm glad."

"Stephen," Uncle Cuyler said, "your concern for the baby is

touching, but I must ask you what you were doing out."

Stephen turned his head away. "I know it was dumb," he said, "but Lydia dared me. She said it was the only way to prove my patriotism."

Uncle Cuyler nodded and pressed his lips together. "And did you?"

"I guess not. And when Lydia finds out I came here, she will really think I'm stupid."

Uncle Cuyler smiled faintly. "You know, Stephen, your mother is my older sister. I know what it's like to have an older sister. I understand how it feels to be the youngest one in the family."

"You do?"

"Sure. I was the baby, and for a long time no one trusted me to do anything. Your mother made me walk home from school with her long after my friends were free to roam around on their own."

"Then you do understand." Stephen laughed, then grabbed his side again. "That really hurts!"

"Do you remember what happened?"

Stephen shook his head. "After I realized what a dumb idea it was to try to find Will, I decided to come straight here. Something hit me in the back of the head."

"My guess is that you got in someone's way. I had to go to the clinic for a potion for the baby, and I found you outside. But I don't know how long you were there."

"Did you get the medicine. . .for the baby?"

"Yes, I gave her a dose, and we'll wait to see what happens."

"You have to take care of her, Uncle Cuyler. Don't worry about me."

"Just lie back and rest, Stephen. I'll send your mother in."

A knock on the front door startled them both. Mama and Aunt Abigail both appeared from the next room, staring at the door with worried frowns. The knocking persisted.

"Step back," Uncle Cuyler said, and he went to the door.

"Who is there?" he called.

"Cuyler? It's me, Richard. Stephen is missing."

Quickly Uncle Cuyler undid the bolt on the door and let his brother-in-law in.

Papa spotted Stephen by the fire immediately. "Stephen, are you all right?" He rushed to his son and knelt next to him. Mama, too, knelt next to Stephen and laid her cool hand on his cheek.

"Uncle Cuyler says my ribs are broken. I'm sorry, Papa. I disobeyed you, and I know it was foolish."

"We'll discuss that later," Papa said. "I'm just glad you're safe."

"I should have known you would miss me. I'm sorry to make you come out when there is so much happening in the streets."

"Actually, it was Lydia who told me that you were gone."

"Lydia?"

Papa nodded. "She told me everything—how she goaded you into going out. We had quite a bit of activity outside the shop this afternoon. So when you didn't come back, she panicked and told me what had happened. I looked all over town for you. I even saw William and started him looking. Then it came to me that this is where you would go—to check on the baby."

"I don't really care about the trial," Stephen said, grimacing with the effort. "Even William cannot convince me that politics are important at a time like this. But the baby—I wanted to be sure she is all right." He looked hopefully at Uncle Cuyler.

"Your uncle will take good care of her," Papa said. "He's a

good doctor. And remember, she's strong—like you, Stephen."

Stephen moved to embrace his father and stopped suddenly. "Ow!"

Papa smiled at him in sympathy. "I think this is one lesson you'll be painfully reminded of for a long time."

CHAPTER 15

Family Reunion

In the morning, the baby's cry was a soft coo. Stephen awoke smiling. But when he tried to sit up, he was forced to surrender to the throbbing headache and the slicing pain in his side. He lay back and listened to the baby's coo and Aunt Dancy's soothing tones, as she hummed and rocked the child across the room from Stephen.

Last night's events were like a bad dream. If he had not found himself sleeping in Aunt Dancy's front room with a knifelike pain cutting through his torso every time he tried to move, Stephen might have thought he had imagined everything. But the pain was real, and the gurgling baby was real.

Stephen knew that the trial of Thomas Preston was only the beginning of Boston's dealings with the men who had been involved that dreadful night more than seven months earlier. The other eight soldiers and the four civilians who had been charged with crimes still awaited trial. The jury agreed that the captain had not given the order for his soldiers to fire. But they had fired, and five men had died. Boston was still determined to hold those who had shot responsible for their actions. William had told his family many things about Samuel Adams. So Stephen knew that the Sons of Liberty were not finished with this case.

It was still very early in the morning. His parents had been persuaded to go home and get some rest with the promise that Uncle Cuyler and Aunt Abigail would look after him. Stephen brightened at the thought that Uncle Cuyler, Aunt Abigail, and Anna had all spent the night at Uncle Ethan and Aunt Dancy's house. They would all be together to celebrate the baby's recovery.

Without moving his body, Stephen turned his head toward his aunt and baby cousin. Aunt Dancy looked calm and content. Her daughter was on the road to recovery. She probably had not paid any attention to the jury's verdict, Stephen decided. Aunt Dancy knew what was important. Her child mattered more than the trial.

Stephen sighed contentedly and dozed once again.

"Stephen? Stephen? Are you awake?"

Without opening his eyes, Stephen turned toward the voice and moaned softly. He had been sleeping deeply and did not want to awaken.

"Stephen, wake up. I have to talk to you."

He forced his eyes open and looked into Lydia's familiar green eyes.

"Papa and Mama said you were hurt. I didn't sleep all night, worrying about you."

"You were worrying about me?" Stephen had not expected that Lydia would be concerned.

"Of course. You're my little brother."

"Oh." He did not know what else to say.

"This is all my fault, Stephen," Lydia said humbly. "I should never have let you leave the shop."

"You practically pushed me out the door," Stephen reminded her.

"But I didn't think you would really go!" Lydia retorted. "I was sure you would be back in three minutes. You have far too much common sense than to stay in the streets during a riot."

Stephen was puzzled. "I thought you wanted me to be more adventuresome."

"That's what I thought, too." Lydia drew her knees to her chest and wrapped her arms around them. "I guess I was counting on you to draw the line between adventuresome and foolish. I'm sorry."

"So you didn't really want me to go out last night?"

"Well," Lydia said thoughtfully, "I did want to know what was going on out there. When you didn't come back right away, I thought maybe you really were going to find something out. But then. . ."

"What happened?"

"There was a street fight right outside the print shop. Some Patriots were lining up against a group of Loyalists. They said awful things to each other! These were people who have been neighbors for years—Sarah Parkenson's father and Agatha Fleming's older brother. Then someone starting swinging a stick. If his friends hadn't had sense enough to stop him, someone would certainly have been hurt. And then I thought about you—how it could be you who got hurt. Then I started to pray."

Tears welled up in Lydia's eyes. She pushed them back with her open palms.

"And I told Papa you were gone. He thought you were in the

back room, but you had been gone for almost an hour by then."

Stephen smiled mischievously. "So you were right about one thing. Papa didn't notice when I left."

"I wish I had been wrong about that. Then he would have made you come back immediately, and you. . .you. . .you wouldn't have been hurt at all. I would understand if you said you could never forgive me."

"Of course I'll forgive you. It's really my own fault that I went out. Besides, I'll be all right. Uncle Cuyler says my ribs will heal quickly because I'm young."

"I'm glad for that. I suppose I'll have to deliver papers by myself until then."

Stephen smiled inwardly at that thought. "And I can just rest at the clinic until I am fully recovered—which could be a very, very long time."

"Don't get any crazy ideas in your head. You can recover at home, and Uncle Cuyler will surely tell us when you are well enough to go back to work."

"You know," Stephen said, "I was at the clinic yesterday when Uncle Ethan came in. At first Uncle Cuyler thought he was there to argue about the jury's verdict. But he was there about the baby. Uncle Cuyler and Uncle Ethan never agree about anything, but when the baby got sick, Uncle Ethan knew where to come. He knew Uncle Cuyler would help."

Lydia laughed. "They actually spent the night under the same roof, and the house is still standing."

Stephen smiled as much as his sore ribs would allow him. "I thought about that a lot during the night. I know that everything William is working for is important—taxes and freedom and everything else he talks about."

"I haven't given up on that," Lydia said.

"I know. It is important. When Mama and Papa talk about how things were when they were growing up, I realize that Boston has been changing my whole life. I don't know when the change will be finished."

"William says the change is only beginning," Lydia said. "He says the Sons of Liberty are willing to go to war against the British if necessary."

"If that happens, I hope that Uncle Cuyler and Uncle Ethan will remember this night," Stephen said, "the night when they forgot about politics because they needed each other."

"It was the baby who brought them together," Lydia said. "An innocent baby who knows nothing of politics or Parliament or the king or colonial assemblies."

Stephen was getting excited. Painfully, he propped himself up on one elbow.

"You're right, Lydia," he said. "It looks like you and I found something to agree on, too."

Aunt Dancy entered the room holding the baby.

"Is she better?" Lydia asked.

"I heard you singing to her earlier," Stephen said. "She wasn't crying."

"She is much better, thanks to your uncle Cuyler." Aunt Dancy smiled at the babe sleeping in her arms.

Lydia reached out and stroked the top of the infant's head. "She's a beautiful baby. I don't think I ever told you that I thought she was beautiful."

Aunt Dancy smiled proudly.

"Does anyone want breakfast?" Aunt Abigail and Anna joined the group in the front room.

"I'm starving," said Lydia most dramatically. "Let's have a huge breakfast."

"Somebody get the boys up to milk the cow," Aunt Dancy said. Anna scurried up the stairs to do her aunt's bidding.

At the sound of a friendly knock on the door, Aunt Abigail opened it. The rest of the Lankford family entered.

"Stephen, you're awake. Good!" Mama went immediately to her son.

"You gave us quite a scare," William said. He shook his finger at Lydia. "I'll talk to you about this later."

"Have you had breakfast?" Aunt Abigail asked.

"No, we came right over here to check on things," Papa said. "I wanted to make sure Stephen and the baby were all right before going to work."

"You'll join us then," Aunt Dancy announced.

Anna was back with the boys. "What is everybody doing here? It's like a holiday family dinner but no holiday," Charles said, rubbing the sleep out of his eyes.

"I think it's wonderful," Anna said. "I'll set the table."

"I would like to offer our patient some toast and tea," Aunt Abigail said, "but I suppose coffee will have to do."

Stephen scowled. He did not like coffee. He missed the tea that his family used to drink before the boycotts.

"I'll put a lot of milk in it," Aunt Abigail assured him.

Aunt Dancy smiled wryly. "I believe that if you look on the top shelf of my pantry, in the back left corner, you will find a tin of tea."

"Really? Tea?" Stephen could hardly believe his good fortune.

"Did someone say tea, or am I still dreaming?" Uncle Cuyler ruffled his uncombed hair with his fingers. Uncle Ethan was right behind him.

"The tea can wait," Lydia announced, rising to her feet. "Stephen and I have something to propose first."

She looked at Stephen, who nodded his agreement.

"I would have thought that the two of you would have learned your lessons about scheming," warned Aunt Abigail, "considering what you have been through in the last few days."

Lydia shook her head vigorously. "This is different. This is not a scheme." She looked around the room, meeting everyone's eyes. When she had their complete attention, she turned to Aunt Dancy and put out her arms. "May I hold Margaret?"

"Margaret?" Aunt Dancy questioned. She glanced at Margaret Lankford.

"The baby," Lydia insisted. "Her name must be Margaret." She took the baby from Aunt Dancy's arms.

Uncle Ethan and Aunt Dancy chuckled. "You have decided the baby's name?"

"Yes, and I'll take her to the minister to christen her myself if I must."

"It's thoughtful of you to want to name her after your grandmother," Margaret Lankford said, "but I do think Uncle Ethan and Aunt Dancy should choose the name for their own daughter."

"But isn't it obvious?" Lydia asked her mother. "Her name must be Margaret. The original Margaret Turner—Kathleen Margaret Turner, your mother and my grandmother—brought this family into being when she had you and Uncle Ethan and

Uncle Cuyler. She wanted our family to love each other. Now her little granddaughter was born on the night of the massacre, and she has brought the family together in spite of our differences— just like Grandma would have wanted."

"I agree with Lydia," Stephen said, grimacing as he pulled himself to a full sitting position. "The baby's name should be Margaret. And she is not named only for our grandmother, but for all the family that came before her."

"Stephen and Lydia have my vote." Will stepped forward and took the baby from Lydia. He studied the infant's face.

"I haven't paid enough attention to you, little one," he said tenderly. "But whatever is ahead for Boston and the rest of the colonies, you will be among those who face the future. It is only right that you should have a name that reminds you of your past."

Aunt Dancy and Uncle Ethan looked at each other and laughed. "Margaret it is," Uncle Ethan said.

"Your grandmother would be proud," said Mama.

Stephen lay back contentedly. Everyone he loved best in the world was in that room right then—even Lydia. War could rage through the streets of Boston, but what mattered most were the people around him right then, no matter what their politics.

But for the moment, he was going to enjoy the benefits that came with being a patient. "I'm ready for that tea and toast now."